P9-DFV-412

ALL THREE STOOGES

ALSO BY ERICA S. PERL

The Capybara Conspiracy

Aces Wild

When Life Gives You O.J.

Vintage Veronica

ALL THREE STOOGES

ERICA S. PERL

ALFRED A. KNOPF New York

THIS IS A BORZOI BOOK PUBLISHED BY ALFRED A. KNOPF

 Published in the United States by Alfred A. Knopf, an imprint of Random House Children's Books, a division of Penguin Random House LLC, New York.

Knopf, Borzoi Books, and the colophon are registered trademarks of Penguin Random House LLC.

Visit us on the Web! rhcbooks.com

Educators and librarians, for a variety of teaching tools, visit us at RHTeachersLibrarians.com

Library of Congress Cataloging-in-Publication Data
Names: Perl, Erica S., author.
Title: All three Stooges / Erica S. Perl.
Description: First edition. | New York : Alfred A. Knopf, 2018. | Summary: While preparing for their bar mitzvahs, comedy-obsessed Noah and Dash find their friendship threatened by a personal tragedy.
Identifiers: LCCN 2017033831 (print) | LCCN 2017006603 (ebook) | ISBN 978-0-399-55175-8 (trade) | ISBN 978-0-399-55177-2 (ebook)
Subjects: | CYAC: Friendship—Fiction. | Bar mitzvah—Fiction. | Comedians—Fiction. | Jews—United States—Fiction. | Family life—Fiction. | Death—Fiction.
Classification: LCC PZ7.P3163 (print) | LCC PZ7.P3163 All 2018 (ebook) | DDC [Fic]—dc23

The text of this book is set in 11.25-point Candida.

Printed in the United States of America
January 2018
10 9 8 7 6 5 4 3 2 1

First Edition

Random House Children's Books supports the First Amendment and celebrates the right to read.

To Teddy Klaus:

Mentor,

Maestro,

Mensch

Chapter One

"Seltzer?"

"Check!"

Dash held up two cans of Fizz Whiz. We always have seltzer, for two reasons. First, it's a classic comedy prop. If you don't know what I'm talking about, google the movie *Three Little Pigskins.* In it, the Three Stooges are all dressed up like women. The best part is when Curly gets seltzer down the front of his dress and goes "Woo-woo-woo!" and then sprays himself in the face. Second, Dash's dad drinks it like water (which, technically, it is), so we make sure we're well stocked for him.

"Popcorn?" I asked.

"Check!" confirmed Dash.

We always have popcorn. Because, duh, who watches movies without popcorn? So with popcorn and seltzer taken care of, we were almost all set. There was just one final requirement.

"Is the doctor in?" I asked.

"Double check!" said Dash, brandishing not one but *two* giant bottles of Dr Pepper.

Not only was Dash's dad, Gil, the coolest guy on the planet, he was a total pushover at the Safeway. Unlike Dash's dad, my moms do not cave to my grocery store demands. Occasionally, if they're feeling generous, they'll get *flavored* seltzer. But at Gil's house, the Dr Pepper flows freely.

"Nnn-okay, drop the beat," I said nasally, doing my best impersonation of a dorky kid impersonating a rapper. "Let's get this party started."

"One sec," said Dash. Then he yelled, "Dad!"

"Hang on, dudes! Be right there," Gil called from upstairs.

"Dad, we're starting without you!" Dash replied. We often had to resort to this kind of deception.

"Hold your horses!" his dad called back.

"Gil, hurry! I can't hold him off much longer!" For Gil's benefit, I stage-whispered, "Dash, don't do it. Don't start without him."

"Too late!" Dash yelled back, cuing up the first video clip. Adam Sandler stared back at us with a triangle play button on his nose. Dash and I both started to fake-laugh maniacally as if we were about to pee our pants over what was on the screen. We paused, listening to see if his dad took the bait.

Still no Gil.

"Close but no cigar," I said.

"All right, proceed to phase two," said Dash.

I nodded. On a silent count of three, we both shouted, "Guess he won't mind if we put on an album!" That almost always worked. Even Dash wasn't allowed to touch Gil's vintage comedy record collection.

"Really, you don't think he'll mind?" I continued loudly.

"Nah, he loves it when we pull records off the shelf and put them back in the wrong places," replied Dash.

"Records? I thought these were Frisbees! Catch!"

"Good one," said Dash, cracking up.

"But, Dash!" I added. "I was just eating peanut butter out of the jar with my hands. Shouldn't I wash them first?"

"No, it's fine. Just wipe them on a record. He'll love that!"

"Dudes. You don't have to yell. I'm right here." Gil stood at the bottom of the stairs, holding bananas and Jiffy Pop. He was wearing his weekend uniform: a Chase Corporate Challenge 5K T-shirt and gray sweatpants. He had perpetual dark circles under his eyes, and even though he didn't have a beard, you could always sort of see the stubble on the bottom of his face through his skin. He also had really hairy arms like a gorilla, so whenever he wore T-shirts, we made monkey noises to mess with him.

"Ooo-ooo-ooo-ooo-ooo!" I said. Because monkey

arms plus bananas. Dash quickly joined in, grabbing a banana from Gil and peeling it. He took a giant bite, then grinned big while scratching himself and jumping around like a monkey. Gil plunked down the popcorn, tossed me a banana, and brandished his like a sword, challenging me to a duel.

"There's something I ought to tell you," he announced, dramatically pausing to switch his weapon to his other hand. I chimed in, quoting *The Princess Bride*, "I'm not left-handed, either!"

Dash laughed, then pointed his half-eaten banana at the tinfoil dome of the Jiffy Pop. "Hey!" he complained. "I thought you were going to let us fry the brain."

"Forgive me, master," said Gil, shifting gears and lurching toward us. "I thought you merely wanted to . . . eat brains."

"Brains! Wah-ha-ha!" I shouted, abandoning my banana sword and staggering toward him, arms out like a zombie. Dash tore into the puffed-up foil and we both grabbed big zombie handfuls. The popcorn was coated with lots of bright yellow fake butter and maybe even fake salt. It tasted like my guinea pig Spud's salt lick. It was awesome.

Dash's dad saw what was happening and kind of dove between the two of us. "Dudes! No zombie popcorn hands on my keyboard! Or peanut butter," he added, giving me a wink. "Back off. I'll drive. Okay, fasten your seat belts. Let's get our SND on."

That was our cue, so Dash and I chimed in and together we all yelled: "Live from the basement, it's Saturday night!"

SND is this game we made up. It's like *SNL*—as in *Saturday Night Live,* but with a *D* for "dudes," obviously—played as a team sport: me and Dash versus Gil. We take turns streaming video clips and riffing on them, awarding points based on who makes who laugh and who finds the best stuff the other team hasn't seen before. Dash and I are undefeated.

Gil hit play and Adam Sandler began strumming his guitar and singing the Chanukah song: "Put on your yarmulke / Here comes Chanukah / So much funukah / To celebrate Chanukah."

Dash and I munched popcorn, spewing it a bit as we sang along. Before long, we got to our favorite verse.

" 'Some people think that Ebenezer Scrooge is,' " sang Dash.

" 'Well, he's not,' " I jumped in. " 'But guess who is?' "

" 'All three Stooges!' " all of us crooned together.

I'm not sure if it was the singing or the salty popcorn, but my mouth had gotten really dry. Which meant that while Dash's dad was cuing up the next clip, I had to chug lots of Dr Pepper fast. Which of course led to another SND tradition:

"Errrrrpp."

"Iddle-biddle baby burp," mocked Dash. He struck a pose and let loose. *"ERRRPPPP!"*

"That was *sort of* like a burp . . . only smaller," I countered before chugging more soda and decimating him. *"ERRRRRRRRRPPPPP!!!!"*

"Noah Cohen!" said Dash, doing his best impression of Mrs. Moseley, who was our fourth-grade teacher. "Always say 'Excuse me' when you pass gas!"

"Well, excuuuuuuuuuse *ERRRRPPPP* me!"

Dash is better than me at a lot of things. For example: soccer, kickball, all sports period, being liked by girls. But I am a far better burper. I also know more comedy routines by heart, even though by all rights he should because his dad is kind of the comedy king. Don't tell my moms, who are mostly awesome, except in the junk food category, but there are times when I would love to trade places with Dash so Gil could be my dad.

"Wait a second . . . hang on . . . *BRAAAAAAAPPPP!"* I cut loose again, strategically aiming my blast at Dash.

"I'll spot you knuckleheads twenty-five extra points if you can go without belching for one minute," said Gil. "Besides, I think it's still my turn."

"Sorry, sorry," we said. Back to the serious business of SND. Gil cued up the lobster scene from *Annie Hall.* Which is my favorite Woody Allen movie, and one of my favorite movies of all time. Even Dash says there's something weird about that, since most Woody Allen movie fans are my moms' age or older.

"Awesome!" I said.

"Dude, you are an old soul," said Gil appreciatively.

In this scene, Woody Allen is trying to cook lobsters, but one escapes behind the refrigerator. Annie Hall is laughing, but Woody is totally freaking out.

" 'Talk to him!' " I said, doing Woody's line in my best Woody voice. " 'You speak shellfish!' "

" 'Maybe if I put a little dish of butter sauce here with a nutcracker, it'll run out the other side,' " added Dash's dad, beating me to Woody's next laugh line.

When the clip ended, we gave Gil fifty points and I knew what had to come next. That's the best part of SND—when you get in the zone and just start riffing on comedy bits, having one lead to another and another. Kind of like a bar mitzvah DJ on a really good night. "Ooh! Ooh! I call *Sleeper* next!" I suggested, ready to go on a Woody Allen roll.

"No, 'Chopper Four'!" said Dash. Dash gets tired of the classics faster than I do.

" 'Chopper Four'?" asked Gil.

"Sklar Brothers," I told him. "You know, they do that bit about how television news teams go nuts when they get a new traffic helicopter."

" 'Chopper Four went down mysteriously in the Hudson River . . . and Chopper Four was first on the scene. Coincidence? Or Chopper Four?' " barked Dash, quoting the clip.

" 'Chopper Four!' " I added, doing the same. " 'The way we see it, we're twice as good as Chopper Two.' "

"Yeah, dudes, I know," said Gil, wrapping one hairy arm around Dash's neck and giving him noogies.

"You've only made me watch it, like, chopper-four-dozen times. I'm not giving you guys any points for it."

" 'Chopper Four'!" we both screamed, sounding just like the Sklar Brothers.

"All right, all right," said Gil, hands up in defeat.

" 'Chopper Four'!" we yelled again triumphantly.

Gil poured himself some seltzer. He chuckled a couple of times at "Chopper 4," but then he slid his chair back and took his cup upstairs. We hit replay when it ended and watched "Chopper 4" twice in a row ("Chopper 8"!). When Gil didn't return, we test-drove a couple more videos to figure out what to wow him with next. Gil loved it when we showed him new stuff, just like we—okay, I—loved it when he showed us old clips we hadn't seen.

"Dad, you coming back?" Dash called upstairs.

"You dudes go ahead," said his dad. "I'm taking a break."

There was still one unopened soda bottle, so I grabbed it and held it up in front of my face. "It is verse zen ve feared," I had it say in my best mad-scientist voice.

"Doctor, is there nothing that can be done?" said Dash.

"Yah," said Dr Pepper. "Zee patient appears to be suffering from . . . lame-o dad-o max-i-mo zyndrome."

"Dr Pepper, didn't they take away your medical license?" Dash accused.

"No! I am ze greatest doctor in all of hee-story!" For emphasis, I tossed the bottle up in the air and caught it. Then I launched it to Dash like a football.

"Ah," said Dash, "so you flew here from Europe? How was your flight?" He tossed it back to me.

"Not bad," I replied, backing up and shaking the bottle before tossing it back. "Except for ze *turbulence.*"

"Oh yeah," said Dash. He caught it and shook it some more before sending it skyward. I missed and it hit the ground again, rolling under Gil's chair. I grabbed it and shook it some more.

"No! I can't take ze pressure!" I said, taking our skit to its inevitable conclusion. "I'm scared I might—"

"Incoming!" yelled Dash, diving for cover under his dad's desk as I unscrewed the cap, drenching both of us. I fell down laughing, landing in a puddle of Pepper. Dash began to slurp the fringe at the edge of the rug for comic effect.

"Maxx! Gross!" I yelled.

Maxx is what me and Dash call each other. It's from one of our earliest forays into comedy: a sketch we called "Mr. Maxx," based on the name of a clothing store near us. We performed it whenever we had an audience of, say, more than one person. Me and Dash were the stars, with my big sister, Enid, and Dash's little brother, Pete, in minor roles.

The sketch would start with me and Dash and Pete

offstage (at my house, this meant in the kitchen). Enid would walk on, dressed as much like a grown-up as possible, and pretend to wait for a bus. Then I'd walk by her wearing a hat. Enid's line was, "I love your hat! Where did you get it?" I'd respond, "Mr. Maxx!" and walk off. Then Dash would walk on and she'd compliment his shirt and ask where he got it. "Mr. Maxx." We'd then do it again and again, naming different articles of clothing, until audience members threatened to leave. "Nice tie!" "Mr. Maxx!" "Nice pants!" "Mr. Maxx!"

Finally, we'd push Pete onstage. The joke depended on him wearing nothing but a diaper. "Hey," Enid would ask him, "what happened to all your clothes?" Pete was then supposed to deliver the punch line: "I'm Mr. Maxx."

Hilarious, right? There was just one problem. Pete was a baby, so he never got it right. Instead, he'd realize he was the center of attention and start giggling. Then he'd pull off his diaper and run in circles, yelling, "Naked man!" Not the kind of sophisticated humor we were aiming for at the time.

In the four years since the dawn of "Mr. Maxx," Dash's and my comic sensibilities have definitely evolved. That said, we still appreciate the inherent genius in, say, turning a soda bottle into a mad scientist or a banana into a sword. Some might call it screwball or goofball, but I think that shows a lack of imagination.

The way I see it, if Gil didn't outgrow that kind of stuff, why should we?

Even so, I confess that I was a little nervous the morning after the Dr Pepper explosion in Gil's office. We hadn't seen him since he "took a break" the night before, and even though we did some mopping, the basement was, well, I think my moms would probably use the word "disaster." Dash and I woke up late and shuffled upstairs, only to find Gil in the kitchen wearing his sweaty running clothes.

"Morning, dudes! Who's ready for breakfast paninis à la G-Force?" Grinning, Gil slid the sandwiches off his George Foreman grill and onto our plates. Dash's dad uses what he calls his G-Force for pretty much all of his cooking. I gotta say, it's pretty versatile.

"Bacon and eggs on waffles?" asked Dash, inspecting his.

"Hey, don't yuck my yum," said Gil, which I'm pretty sure he picked up from my moms. "Ketchup? Hot sauce? Maple syrup?"

"Sure, sure, and sure!" I said. Dash passed me a glass full of leftover semi-flat Dr Pepper to wash the food down. Gil raised his coffee cup and toasted us with it, then turned his attention to the *Washington Post.*

In other words, it was a totally typical post-sleepover morning. If I close my eyes, I can feel how warm and sunny Gil's kitchen was. I can smell the waffles and bacon and coffee. And I can remember how happy I was that I had nowhere to be for hours and that after breakfast we could pick up right where we left off showing each other comedy clips.

But the thing I remember most about that morning is the Magic 8 Ball. Dash bought it for his dad, and it lived on Gil's desk next to his computer. Whenever Dash was at the keyboard pulling up videos, I would ask it a question. And then I'd shake it and check the answer. And shake it again if I didn't like the answer. And keep shaking it until I did like the answer or it was my turn to take the keyboard and drive.

Early that morning, when we woke up, I asked it a question: "Magic 8 Ball, am I going to become a famous comedian?"

REPLY HAZY, TRY AGAIN.

I asked again.

REPLY HAZY, TRY AGAIN.

And again. REPLY HAZY, TRY AGAIN.

"This stupid thing is stuck," I told Dash.

"Let me see it," he said, and I tossed it to him. "Magic 8 Ball, is Noah going to bomb as a comedian?" He gave it a shake, looked, then laughed out loud.

WITHOUT A DOUBT.

"Give me that!" I said, grabbing it out of his hands. While he wasn't looking, I repeated *my* question, silently.

REPLY HAZY, TRY AGAIN.

"Stupid ball," I said, then rolled it across the room, and we went upstairs for breakfast. I forgot all about that Magic 8 Ball until the next day. And I didn't think much about it even then, because I just figured the next time I was over, I'd try again.

That's because I didn't know there wouldn't be a next time.

Chapter Two

The following Tuesday afternoon, at three-thirty, I was clinging to a pole on the number 31 bus, trying to stay vertical as it hit every single pothole on Wisconsin Avenue. I waved my free arm wildly like you might do if you were, say, a person who actually wanted a teacher to call on you.

"So get this," I said when I finally had everyone's attention. I love having everyone's attention. Everyone being Deena Leon, Jared Rosenfeld, Adam Metz-Peterson, Eli Webb, Sarah Patel, Noa Cohen, and all the other kids who go to my school and ride the bus to Hebrew school with me every Tuesday afternoon. I feel bad for the kids like Dash who go to middle school in Bethesda. They carpool instead of riding the bus, so they miss my weekly stand-up routines.

Noa shot Deena a look and groaned before I even started the joke. Undaunted, I launched into the setup. "Two old ladies are at a fancy hotel," I said, ignoring both Noa and an old lady who turned around to glare at me. "And one of them says, 'The food here is really terrible.' And the other one goes, 'Yeah, I know. And such small portions!' "

I'm guessing that with all the bus noise, no one could hear the punch line. Which explains why I didn't get a big laugh. I let go of the pole to do a rim shot for emphasis, but the bus lurched over another pothole and I almost fell over. I decided to switch to bus jokes. Always good to cater to your audience's interests.

"The number thirty-one is so slow," I tried, "a cop pulled it over to give it a parking ticket!"

"I wish it went slower," said Adam, missing my joke completely.

"Yeah," agreed Jared. "The longer it takes, the less time we have to spend at Hebrew school."

Everyone laughed, which was stupid because it wasn't even a joke! I laughed, too, because I didn't want everyone to know that, unlike them, I actually look forward to Hebrew school.

Don't get me wrong—I don't *love* it. But since Dash and I don't go to the same school anymore, Tuesday afternoons are the only time I get to hang out with him during the week. Plus, the teachers are kind of okay, and then there's Rabbi Fred. In addition to being a rabbi, he's the education director at our temple, which means he's like the principal of Hebrew school. His name fits him perfectly because he looks a lot like an older Fred Flintstone. He has white hair and a big nose and twinkly eyes like he's in a good mood all the time, which he mostly is.

One of my moms, Karen, says Rabbi Fred is a mensch. The first time she said it, I was confused because it's also what she calls the guy at the garage who works on Frau Blue Car (that's our Volkswagen's name—it's a *Young Frankenstein* joke). It sounded so much like "wrench" that I thought maybe she meant Rabbi Fred was some kind of Jewish mechanic. I soon learned that "mensch" and "wrench" have nothing to do with each other. (I don't think Rabbi Fred has any idea how to fix a car—he rides his bike, mostly.) The closest synonym for "mensch" is probably "a good guy," but Rabbi Fred is more than that. He's a deeply good person through and through. And in case you're wondering, "mensch"—even though it has the word "men" in it—is not a gender-specific term. Girls can be mensches, too.

But not all of them are. Take Noa Cohen. Please!

Noa Cohen has a big head with a big mouth and big teeth and big hair—long, curly red hair. She's kind of a Hermione type, except no wand, and Jewish. But that's not the reason she's my nemesis. This is: her name *sounds* exactly like my name, although I hasten to point out to you that she does *not* have my exact same name. She's Noa Cohen, and I'm Noah Cohen.

Cohen is one of the most common Jewish last names on the planet. It's mine because it's Karen's last name. My other mom is Jenny Haus. My sister, Enid, is a Haus because Jenny used to be married to a guy named Howard Haus, who is Enid's dad. Then they got divorced, and Jenny and Karen fell in love and had me and the rest is history. When my moms got married, they talked about hyphenating, but they couldn't stop laughing over Cohen-Haus sounding like "co-hen-house," so they ended up just leaving everything as it was. Though for the wedding invitations, they did use a picture I drew of a chicken coop, with four smiling chickens in it to represent the four of us: me, Enid, Karen, and Jenny.

For reasons that make exactly no sense to me, the fact that Noa and I have similar names makes people think we are brother and sister. Which is nuts, because who would do that to their kids? Plus, Noa Cohen and I are not alike in any way. For example:

1. Noa always hands in her homework on time. It's kind of her thing. As for me, I almost always do my homework. I just sometimes find it at the bottom of my backpack when I'm standing on the stairs of the number 31 bus looking for my DC One Card so the driver will let me on.
2. Teachers love Noa. The same cannot always be said about me. (It has been

pointed out to me by my moms that this may have something to do with the whole not-handing-in-my-homework thing.)
3. We're both Jewish, but technically I am only 50 percent Jewish, same as Dash. For him, it's his dad, and for me, it's my mom Karen. Guess who's 100 percent Jewish and likes to make sure everyone knows it?
4. Noa is *not* funny. I, on the other hand, am hilarious.

Just to be clear, I can think of tons of girls that are funny. Like Tina Fey, who is one of the funniest people on the planet. She wrote all that stuff for *SNL* before she was even on the show, and then she made tons of funny shows and movies and wrote hilarious sketches for herself and other people. And she wrote the book *Bossypants,* which is a riot. I got the audiobook for Chanukah last year, and I listened to it so many times I could pretty much recite the whole thing. Here's the point: Noa is no Tina Fey. She's like the anti-Fey.

I knew this from the moment I first met Noa, a million years ago, at our neighborhood playground. I was minding my own business, stomping around the sandpit with my dinosaurs—I was *really* into dinosaurs at the time—and someone's fairy princess whatever-it-was got in my way. The next thing I knew, three moms were running at me, yelling my name.

Two-thirds of those moms were mine, and getting yelled at by them was nothing new. But the third mom was a total stranger, so that part was confusing. It turned out she wasn't yelling at me. She was yelling *my* name at this little girl with a big, open mouth who was screaming louder than all three moms put together.

To the best of my recollection, here's what happened next:

Other mom: Noa! Sweetie! Are you okay? Did the mean, terrible boy ruin your bee-yoo-tee-ful creation?

Noa: Wahhhhhhhhhhhh!!! [She was a drama queen, even then.]

Karen: Wait a second, her name is Noah? He's Noah, too.

Other mom: Yes, but it's *N-o-a,* no *h.* Noa Cohen.

Jenny: Did you say Cohen?

Karen: That's his last name, too!

Other mom: No way.

My moms: Way! [They actually say this, like in *Wayne's World*. I think it's old-people slang.]

For a couple of happy years following that day at the playground, I didn't see Noa. Then she showed up in my kindergarten class to steal my cubby (she denies this, but who do you think would remember it better, me or her?). And she's been in my class every year ever since. Every year! It's like some sort of bad, evil, twisted joke in the main office. "Hey, let's put Noah Cohen and Noa Cohen in the same class *again*!"

On the first day of fifth grade, I called Dash to tell him to guess who was in my class again, surprise, surprise.

"George Foreman," said Dash. "You know, the grill guy."

Dash's mom had just moved out, and Dash's dad had just bought the first in a series of G-Forces. According to Gil, it was fine that Dash's mom took most of the kitchen equipment with her—with his G-Force, he was all set. George Foreman made me think of George from *Seinfeld,* which is one of my favorite shows of all time.

"Ha-ha. Very funny," I said flatly, thinking about the episode where George tells Jerry how his gym teacher used to call him Can't-stand-ya instead of Costanza. Even though I wish it were the other way around, Dash is more the Jerry type and I'm more the George. Fifth grade didn't get off to a great start. Dash's mom had made Dash transfer to a school near her apartment in Bethesda. And it felt like everyone had grown over the summer—except me. Noa Cohen was suddenly a whole head taller than me.

"That wasn't a guess," said Dash. "I just thought it might make you feel better to know that George Foreman has five sons named George."

"What's your point?" I asked. I wondered if his dad's new grill had come with a *George Foreman Fun Facts* brochure.

"I dunno. Things could be worse?" said Dash.

"This is my *sixth* year in the same class with Noa," I informed him. "There's no way things could be worse."

Guess what? I was wrong. I found this out a few weeks later, at Hebrew school, when we received our dates-and-deets sheets. That's a form you get when you're ten that tells you stuff about your future bar or bat mitzvah, like the date and your bar mitzvah partner—that's the kid you'll share your bar mitzvah with if there aren't enough dates to go around. My sheet said:

Noah Cohen

Torah portion: *Acharei Mot*

Tutor: Rabbi Fred Klein

Bar mitzvah date: April 30 (7th-grade school year)

Bar mitzvah partner: Noa Cohen

Noa Cohen? Seriously?! As my bar mitzvah partner? What had I done to deserve this fate?

There was only one person who could possibly help. And that person was Rabbi Fred. So I took my sheet to his office. I gave a quick knock and waited for him to answer.

Rabbi Fred's office is one of those places where everywhere you look, there's something cool. He has masks hanging on his walls and a framed baseball jersey and a huge shofar horn with three curls in it. But my favorite thing in his office is something he calls his water feature.

It sits on a bookcase next to Rabbi Fred's desk and

looks like a faucet you'd see on the side of a house for a hose to be hooked up to, only the back part isn't connected to a house or anything. It just hangs in the air. Yet there's water, real water, coming out of the faucet and pouring into a metal bucket of rocks sitting below it to catch the water. The water is always on, which used to make me have to pee. With practice, I've gotten better at tuning it out. But when I saw it the first time, I thought it was the coolest thing ever because the faucet isn't connected to anything. The water just flows and flows, but it's like magic because the faucet isn't hooked up and is just, like, suspended there in midair. It looks perfectly balanced, like you could reach over and turn off the water and then the faucet would just fall on the floor. Also, the water never overflows the metal bucket, which makes no sense, either.

Dash was the one who figured out how it worked. The next time I got a chance, I stuck a finger into the stream and confirmed that his theory was right: there was a little tube hidden inside the stream to carry the water right back to where it started.

Rabbi Fred loved to ask people what they thought the magic faucet symbolized. He kept a list on his bulletin board, and when he heard a new interpretation, he'd add it to his list. And he'd give whoever thought of the idea a Tootsie Pop, too! So the day I saw Dash with a Tootsie Pop, I ran in to see what his reason was. There it was, seventh on the list:

What Meanings Can We Derive from This Water Feature?

1. Inspiration can come from anywhere or nowhere.
2. Faith has no beginning and no end.
3. Love flows like water.
4. People need G-d, like water, to live.
5. Torah connects people in an endless cycle.
6. Judaism <u>rocks</u>! [Apparently, this was Noa Cohen's contribution. She bragged to everyone about it later, pulling out her Tootsie Pop to say, "Get it? Because there are rocks?" Rabbi Fred liked this so much he underlined the word "rocks" and doled out an exclamation point, which is the kind of thing teachers do for Noa all the time.]
7. Stay hydrated!

Like Noa, Dash got an exclamation point. I was actually more jealous of that than the Tootsie Pop.

The door opened.

"You rang?" said Rabbi Fred dramatically. He always says that, even though there's no bell to ring.

"Um, yeah," I said. "I was wondering if it's possible to, uh, change something?" I handed him my sheet.

"This wouldn't happen to be about your bar mitzvah partner?" asked Rabbi Fred, smiling.

"Possibly," I admitted.

Rabbi Fred gave me a sympathetic smile and handed the sheet back to me. "I'm sorry, Noah. Our policy is that after the dates are assigned, we leave any necessary schedule swaps to the families," he said. "But please know that it wasn't purposeful. If it were, don't you think we would have given you *Noach* as a Torah portion?"

He laughed. I didn't.

"Sorry, just a little biblical humor. All kidding aside," Rabbi Fred continued, "every year, we look at the calendar, line up the class in birth order, and assign the available service spots in the order the kids were born."

He went to his bookcase, scrutinized the shelves, selected a slim book, and handed it to me. *Parashat Acharei Mot,* it read on the front.

"Here," he said. "Check it out: it's your parsha."

A parsha is a Torah portion. There's one for each week, all year long. Some parshas are pretty well known, like *Yitro,* which is the one where Moses receives the Ten Commandments. I listened patiently while Rabbi Fred told me that my parsha, *Acharei Mot,* was from Leviticus. In it, God tells Aaron all the things he (Aaron, that is) has to do to help the community make things right after something bad happens. One of the things is taking a goat and sending it out into the wilderness. "You've heard of a scapegoat?" asked Rabbi Fred. "You know, someone who gets blamed for something he didn't do? People think this is where that expression originated."

"Cool," I said. What I was actually thinking was, *There's no point in starting to learn this particular parsha quite yet. If I switch dates, it'll be a different portion.*

Unfortunately, I soon found out that in our whole b'nei mitzvah class, no one was willing to switch with me. So then I got the brilliant idea that maybe I could talk Noa into switching her date with Dash and he could be my partner instead of her.

"His date isn't until the following fall," I pointed out to her. "So you'd have tons more time to get ready!"

"For your information, Noah, my mom has known my date for over a year," said Noa. "We needed to get it early to make sure it didn't conflict with my cousin Luke's. It's his bar mitzvah year, too."

"Why didn't you tell me?" I asked.

"I knew it was my date. I didn't know it was *your* date," she said, like I was the one being stupid. She turned to go, flipping her curly red hair in my face.

"Wait, Noa—" I tried to run after her, but I slipped and fell and landed in a big pile of underwear.

Yes, underwear. Every year at our temple, the sixth graders do an underwear drive for the homeless. That year, the theme was "Winter UNDERland," so the sixth graders had built a display involving a giant snowman constructed out of bags of donated socks and underwear. After they did this, more people continued to drop off plastic bags of donated socks and undies. They were all over the floor by where the snowman's feet would be if snowmen had feet. So now the poor snowman—or underwear-man, I guess I should say—was sort of melting into a gigantic puddle of undies. And when I slid on a plastic bag, I landed in the underwear pond myself.

Noa could have reached out and helped me up. But instead, she used her hands to cover her mouth because she had started giggling. And then Deena and Sadie and Sarah and Elena and all the other girls came up the stairs and they started laughing, too. And when I tried to stand up, I slipped and fell down again, which made them laugh harder. Just then, Rabbi Jake came in. To his credit, he did fish me out of the underwear pond. I started to thank him, but he cut me off, smiling.

"Whatever you have to say, Noah, keep it *brief,*" he said, setting everyone off again.

Great, I thought. *Everyone's a comedian now.*

Except me, apparently. Because there was nothing funny about being stuck with Noa Cohen for all eternity.

Chapter Three

The thing about the dates-and-deets sheet is that you get it in fifth grade, but then everyone forgets all about it. Until the beginning of seventh grade, that is, when the mitzvah project meeting takes place.

"Why do we need a meeting?" I whispered to Dash. The way mitzvah projects usually work at our temple is that each kid does his or her own project, like volunteering. Dash shrugged and looked longingly out the open window. It was a warm September afternoon and we were in the temple library. I could hear the fifth and sixth graders outside, allegedly decorating the sukkah. I could tell that Dash and I were thinking the same thing—that maybe if there weren't many questions, the meeting would end early and we could go outside, too.

Rabbi Jake, who's like a junior rabbi, got everyone's

attention by announcing, "This year, we're trying something new." Rabbi Fred and our cantor, Phyllis, beamed like Rabbi Jake was their son and he had gotten straight A's on his report card.

None of us kids beamed back. At my house, "trying something new" often means dinner will be something like tempeh kebabs with cashew curry. Which is actually not all that bad, but it's not as good as veggie burgers. Did I mention that when Enid became a vegan, we became a no-meat house, though the rest of us still eat cheese and eggs?

"As you guys know," Rabbi Jake said, "Rabbi Douglas is on a 'rabbatical' in Israel this year, so I'm stepping up to help Rabbi Fred with the mitzvah project. Before Rabbi Douglas left, he told me that we've gotten feedback from previous b'nei mitzvah classes. Apparently, the mitzvah project piece of the experience often feels like a chore. Something you have to do to check it off a list." I couldn't really argue with him there—I am not a big fan of chores, like cleaning Spud's cage. "This made us think," he continued. "How could we use this time better to create opportunities for collaboration, community learning, and—dare I say it—*fun*?"

Rabbi Fred and Phyllis nodded in agreement. Around the room, kids were looking at each other nervously. I could tell that a lot of us were expecting the next thing to come out of Rabbi Jake's mouth to be a pitch for all of us to spend our weekends cleaning up the overgrown weeds lining the Capital Crescent Trail. So I was surprised by what came next.

"We've decided to let you guys come up with a theme and have each of you research something or someone that's connected to the theme. Then we'll have an all-community event for you guys to present your work and celebrate all that you learned."

Noa raised her hand, a look of concern on her face. "How is that a mitzvah?" she asked.

"Well," said Rabbi Fred. "Think of it as a gift you'll give to the community: sharing your time and your knowledge. And also, we'd like you to identify a charity that's somehow related to your theme so that you can raise funds and provide a grant."

More hands went up.

"So, we can pick *anything*? Like . . . skateboarding?" asked Chris Stern.

"We're not saying no to any subject per se," said Rabbi Jake, spreading his hands wide and casting a nervous glance in the direction of Rabbi Fred.

"Here are the basic parameters," explained Rabbi Fred. "One, we're just going to ask you to look at your topic through a distinctly Jewish lens. So, for example, that might mean profiling famous Jewish skateboarders."

"I'll take 'Famous Jewish Skateboarders' for two hundred!" I called out, *Jeopardy!*-style. I got a couple of laughs for that.

"Or maybe an Israeli-Palestinian skateboarding club," suggested Phyllis.

Rabbi Fred nodded. "Exactly. If there is such a thing. Is this making sense? Two, you're going to need to work in teams, ideally of three or four. And, three, everyone needs to vote, and whichever theme gets the most votes wins. Majority rules. Okay? Any questions?"

Around the room, hands went up. Including mine, but Rabbi Jake called on Maya Edelstein instead. She wanted to know if we could do Harry Potter. Rabbi Jake smiled. "I actually thought about that one," he said. "I think yes, and there are several ways you could do it. One would be to create a midrash for some of the ethical issues that the characters in the series confront, and figure out what the Torah might say about them." When Maya looked disappointed, he added, "We can talk more about that later. Midrashim can be kind of like fan fiction." She perked up at the sound of that.

Rabbi Jake fielded several other questions. Finally, he called on me.

"Do you have to work with your bar mitzvah partner?" I asked. I meant it to sound more casual, but I had been waiting so long that the question just launched itself like a rocket. Noa glared at me. She looked like a bee getting ready to sting.

"You can *choose* to work with your bar mitzvah partner," Rabbi Jake said, flipping my question rather than answering it. "And/or anyone else in the b'nei mitzvah class. The whole point here is creative collaboration."

He paused and looked around the room for other questions.

"Noah," said Rabbi Fred, pointing at me when Noa and I both turned, "when we shift gears, can I see you?"

The minute our brainstorming time began, Rabbi Fred led me out to the hallway to suggest that I work on being more sensitive to the feelings of others, as well as more open-minded. "It's been my experience," he advised, "that sometimes, when you least expect it, people can surprise you." I told him I would, and the minute he released me, I ran back into the library, where I found Dash deep in conversation with . . . Noa? She was telling him some long story about going to some museum and getting to see some attic.

To demonstrate that I could be sensitive to others (and open-minded), I didn't interrupt her. However, all around the room, I could see that kids were excitedly discussing project ideas. Noa kept right on talking to Dash. Finally, I couldn't wait any longer. When Noa took a breath, I caught Dash's eye and blurted out, "Jewish comedy! That could be the overall theme and we could do *our* part on *Seinfeld.* Awesome, right?"

"Noah, come on," said Noa. "I was just saying to Dash that we should suggest Anne Frank, or the Holocaust in general, as a theme. I think that's a lot more important than skateboards or *comedy.*"

She said it with more than a little disdain, and to my total amazement, Dash opened his mouth and said, "She's got a point."

"Maxx!" I said pointedly. "How can you say that? We're talking *Seinfeld* here. No offense, but the Holocaust?" I saw the look of horror on Noa's face and quickly added, "As a topic, I mean! Sure, it's *important,* obviously, but we've been studying it forever. It's kind of been done to death."

"Noah!" yelled Noa.

"Not like that!" I said. "You know what I mean."

"We'll see what the rabbis have to say about your idea," said Noa snippily.

As if on cue, Rabbi Jake said, "Guys, guys!" and clapped to get everyone's attention. Then he held out one hand, palm up, and Chris Stern sullenly surrendered the fingerboard deck he'd been playing with. "Okay, I love the energy, and I'm hearing some great ideas here. Who wants to share some possible themes?"

Noa raised her hand and waved it like a flag. When Rabbi Jake called on her, she tried to sell her idea about the Holocaust and making a model of Anne Frank's house and all the other cool stuff people could do. A couple of the kids nodded like it wouldn't be the worst idea in the world, but the response seemed pretty lukewarm.

"Okay, good suggestion," said Rabbi Jake, putting it on the list. "Anyone else?"

I raised my hand again. Other kids got called on, and more ideas were added to the list: skateboarding, Harry Potter, horses, Jews in the NFL. Finally, Rabbi

Jake shot me a stern look. Since no one else's hand was up, he had no choice but to call on me.

"I think a good theme would be comedy. Jewish comedy."

"Interesting," said Rabbi Jake, and he said it in a way that sounded like he actually meant it. Rabbi Jake isn't, like, ha-ha funny, but he definitely shows signs of having a sense of humor.

Encouraged, I went on. "Yeah, so there are lots of famous Jewish comedians that we all know, like Jerry Seinfeld, and Ben Stiller, and—"

"Amy Schumer's Jewish, too," added Deena.

"Right!" I said. "And Jon Stewart and Andy Samberg . . ."

"Adam Sandler," yelled Chris.

"Tina Fey!" called someone else.

"Actually, Tina Fey's not Jewish," I said, "but lots of other comedians are." That got everyone buzzing, but I knew I needed the rabbis on board, so I quickly added, "Plus, we could learn about a whole bunch of classic comedians that not many people our age have heard of, like Henny Youngman . . . "

"Groucho Marx, Billy Crystal, Jackie Mason," said Rabbi Fred. "You know, Noah, you might just have something there."

"Thanks!" I said, trying not to be too in-your-face about it to Noa. The noise level in the room rose as everybody started arguing about their favorite comedians and who was funnier and who was Jewish or not. We took a vote, with paper ballots and everything, but it was totally obvious that my idea was a grand-slam win. I was shocked and totally stoked. I had never won anything before, not even Class Clown in our sixth-grade yearbook, because this kid named Karl Shevchenko was an actual clown, like from a circus family. If the kids at my school weren't so literal, I would've won that title, easy. But this was even better!

Once it was decided, we were supposed to break up into groups to decide which comedians we wanted to study. Someone even suggested that we should call the all-community event the Kings and Queens of Comedy Cabaret and all dress up as famous Jewish comedians.

"Quick," I told Dash, "let's sign up for *Seinfeld* before someone else takes it. We can be Jerry and George."

"Sure," he said. "And Noa could be Elaine."

"Yeah! Wait, what?" I couldn't believe my ears. "Dude, Rabbi Jake said we didn't have to work with our bar mitzvah partners."

"I know, but it's supposed to be teams of three, right? Plus, I think she's kind of bummed about her idea not getting picked."

I glanced over. I could see he had a point. Noa was sitting there reading a book while everyone talked excitedly around her. I knew it was the right thing to do, but I couldn't help feeling a little irritated. Dash didn't know what it was like to always have to be stuck with her every single time.

And then I had my second brilliant idea of the day.

"I know!" I said. "Let's not do *Seinfeld*. I have an even better idea. Come on."

Dash followed me over to Noa, and I jumped right in.

"Hey, Noa," I said. "Dash and I were hoping you'd form a team with us. We have a great idea and we want you to be part of it."

"You do?" said Noa, looking up with excitement. But then, almost as if she smelled something fishy, she closed her book and eyed me suspiciously. "What's the idea?"

"We can do the Three Stooges!" I said. "All three of them were Jewish. Four if you count Shemp, which I don't." I added that last bit for completeness because, technically, Shemp was a Stooge, too, even though he wasn't one of the big three: Larry, Curly, and Moe.

"The Three Stooges? Aren't they those guys who hit each other and stuff?" asked Noa.

"I mean, sometimes," I said. "But they're really funny. You'll love them!"

Of course I knew that there was no way she would. Dash and I had watched a lot of Stooges clips, most of which involved the Stooges slapping each other or poking each other in the eyes or crashing through a three-level bunk bed. None of which seemed to me like things Noa would like.

"Plus," I added, "the Stooges made lots of movies before and during World War Two. They even made fun of Hitler. So there's history there."

"I guess that could be interesting," admitted Noa. I knew she'd take the bait! I ran over to Rabbi Jake's whiteboard and signed us up to seal the deal.

The next day, Noa confronted me in the hall at school.

"Moe, Larry, and *Curly*?" she said pointedly.

"Yeah?" I said.

"I suppose I'm Curly?"

"Why?" I asked.

"Because, duh!" She leaned down so we were nose to nose and grabbed a big handful of her thick, curly red hair for emphasis. I couldn't help it—I pulled away and started to laugh.

"What's so funny?" said Noa.

"Curly . . . ," I said, choking out the word between laughs. "Curly . . . is the . . . bald one!"

"No, he's not," said Noa.

"Yeah, he is," I said. "Did you even, like, watch any?"

"I googled them," said Noa. "There was a picture."

"You can't understand the Stooges by looking at a picture. You have to see them in action." I thought quickly. "How about this? Next week, Dash and I can show you some of our favorite clips at Hebrew school. It'll make sense then."

"I doubt that," said Noa before stomping off to class.

My plan was working! And soon we would settle this once and for all. We would show Noa the Three

Stooges and she would hate them and refuse to work with us.

Unless . . . she liked them?

No, that wasn't possible.

The following Tuesday, Dash and I got special permission from Rabbi Fred to use some of our skills class time for our research. So instead of working on our chanting, we sat around a screen in the temple library and introduced Noa to the Three Stooges. Noa was taking the whole thing really seriously. She had her notebook and pencil case out, ready to take notes. That seemed like a surefire way to suck the fun out of any endeavor, but since we were getting out of skills class to watch videos, I wasn't going to say anything. We led off with *I Can Hardly Wait,* one of my favorites. It starts with the Stooges breaking into what looks like a safe but is actually a refrigerator. It felt weird to be watching it during daylight hours, not to mention watching it with someone other than just Dash and Dash's dad.

Dash clicked play, and the Stooges came to life, making breakfast while slapping and punching each other and calling each other names. I started giggling before anything even happened because I knew what was in store for us. Within the first five minutes, Curly ends up putting mustard all over Moe's hand and trying to eat it like a sandwich. Then Moe dunks Larry's face into a pot of boiling water. Dash and I love it when

Larry grabs his nose and wails, "Ohh! You burnt my little bugle!"

"Whaddya think, Curly?" I asked Noa. I had told Dash about her thinking Larry was Curly because of his curly hair—we had a good laugh about that.

Noa hit pause and turned to face us.

"You think *this* is funny?" she said, looking appalled.

"Yeah!" I said, thrilled that the clip was having exactly the effect I'd hoped for.

"It's funny because you know what's going to happen," Dash explained, "then you watch it happen and you see them react to it happening."

"But they're hurting each other," said Noa. I almost thought she was going to cry. "How can you laugh at that?"

"No one's really getting hurt," Dash reassured her. "It's slapstick. It's all choreographed, like wrestling. Or ballet. My dad showed us lots of clips like this. This kind of humor goes back to Shakespeare or even earlier. Wait, take a look at this."

He pulled up another clip. Not the Three Stooges, but an old silent film called *Mr. Flip,* which includes the first pie-in-the-face gag. It's about a guy who keeps misbehaving with women, and the women make sure he gets what's coming to him. They poke scissors under his chair, they spray him with shaving cream and seltzer. And, of course, he gets a pie in the kisser.

"See," said Dash.

"Uh-huh," said Noa, her eyes fixed on the screen. You could tell the fact that there were women doing pranks to get a guy back for being a jerk made it better for her. But that wasn't the point, so I quickly pulled up another Stooges clip.

"What's with all the *nyuk-nyuk-nyuks* and *woo-woo-woos*?" Noa asked.

"It's like a cappella sound effects," said Dash. "They did a lot of stuff like that to make the humor really exaggerated." He reached over to give me the two-finger eye gouge, but I pulled back and went "Woo-woo-woo!" Then I bent forward to set up that thing where you fling your arms out to fake slap the other guy—

At which point I hit Noa's pencil case, sending her pencils and pens flying in all directions.

"Noah!" wailed Noa, standing up abruptly.

"I'm sorry!" I yelped, diving for the floor.

"You've got to be more careful," she scolded, even though I was already on my hands and knees scrambling to collect her things. "If we're going to do this, we have to make sure we deliver a really polished presentation. I don't have time for messing around. My bat mitzvah is in six months."

"So is *my* bar mitzvah," I reminded her, handing over everything I'd collected off the floor. "Wait, you still want to work with us?"

"Of course," she said.

"But . . . you don't like the Stooges," I said, confused.

Noa seemed to take this as a compliment. "It's true, I have a more sophisticated sense of humor," she boasted. "But I could see how others might find them funny. Plus, they're historical, so there's that."

"Well, *that* went well," I said sarcastically to Dash after Hebrew school. We were standing out in front of the temple, waiting for our rides home.

"It was your idea," Dash reminded me.

"Yeah, but if you hadn't been so encouraging about her stupid idea, I wouldn't have had to come up with it in the first place," I argued.

Just then, I saw Gil walking up. He gave me kind of a salute, then gestured with his head toward where his car was parked. There were a lot of parents coming and going, but no sign of Frau Blue Car yet.

"Don't blame me," called Dash, jogging down the steps to join his dad, then hanging back to get in position. "Blame my sidekick." He went to kick his dad in the butt jokingly. It was a bit they often did to each other. Gil would see it coming and grab Dash's foot in midair. Dash would end up hopping up and down, howling, while his dad held on with one hand and tried to give him noogies with the other. But today Gil didn't even seem to notice when Dash kicked him.

"All right, kiddo. Enough clowning around. Let's go," said Gil. "See ya, Noah."

I stood there, surprised. Dash's dad usually called me dude, not Noah. "Wait, did my moms say anything to you about driving me?" I asked.

Gil shook his head. "Do you need a ride? If you do, hop in. I'm just in a bit of a rush, and I need to get Dash to his mom's."

"Nah, I'm okay. I just— Wait, never mind." I saw Jenny waving from where she was double-parked across the street. I called out to Dash, who was already in the car, "Hey, Maxx. We're still on for Saturday night, right?"

I asked because sometimes Dash bails on me for no reason. To my relief, Dash said, "Sure thing, Maxx."

But that Saturday afternoon, I got a text:

Maxx: Can't do sleepover. Sry!

I replied:

Me: Maxx! Y not?

In return, I got:

Maxx: My dad needs me here.

What was that supposed to mean? Maybe he needed Dash to clean his room or help reorganize the comedy album collection. I texted back:

Me: What for? I can help!

No response. I kicked my desk in frustration.

"Woink! Woink, woink, woink!" Spud's cage sits on my desk, and he often misinterprets seismic disturbances. I reached down and picked him up.

"Sorry, boy," I told him, scratching his ears. "There's no earthquake. It's just Dash being Dash."

Spud seemed disappointed by the news. He tried to eat my shirt to console himself, so I put him back and gave him some timothy hay instead.

"Razz? Hey, Razz," I called, shaking my pencil cup, which my cat sometimes mistakes for the sound of the treat canister. Everyone knows quality pet time is the best remedy for when your best friend ditches you for no reason. Everyone except for Raspberry, apparently. I wandered out to the living room and gave the cup a shake. Jenny was on the couch, drinking tea and watching basketball. She looked up at the sound.

"Cat treats?" she said. "No, thanks. I'm trying to cut back."

"Have you seen Razzie?"

"Nope," she said. "But the *Guinness World Records* people were just here looking for her, too. Something about crowning her the World's Most Aloof Cat?"

I sat down next to her on the couch and sighed dramatically.

"Lemme guess, Dash changed his mind about the sleepover?" Jenny asked.

"He didn't change his mind," I corrected her. "He just can't do it after all. His dad needs him. Whatever that means."

"Bummer," said Jenny. I nodded. We both sat there while they instant-replayed a layup shot several times.

"You hungry?" she asked.

"Always."

So when Karen got home, they took me to Z-Burger for an actual meat hamburger. Enid was at a friend's, so we didn't even have to listen to a meat-is-murder lecture on our way out the door. But all those lectures must have taken root in my brain, because after we got home, it felt like a big lump of dead cow was camping out in my stomach. Thankfully, the World's Most Aloof Cat finally slunk out of Enid's room to sit on my belly. And since I couldn't sleep, my moms let me stay up and watch *SNL.* We streamed it on Jenny's laptop and watched it together, all three of us curled up in their room in what I used to call the big bed. It wasn't as good as SND would have been, but it did help a little.

What helped the most, though, was the text I got from Dash at midnight:

Maxx: Next weekend i promise!!!

Chapter Four

All week long, I prepared for SND. Dash wasn't at Hebrew school on Tuesday—a dentist appointment, apparently—so I had to plan our strategy on my own. I watched tons of comedy clips and made lists of the best ones—guaranteed pee-your-pants-funny hits, one and all. I packed my overnight bag three days early. I spent my allowance on Dr Pepper. I even cleaned Spud's cage ahead of time so when it came time to go to Dash's house, my moms couldn't notice it hadn't been done and delay my departure.

Finally, at long last, it was Saturday evening. It was just about time for me to head over when I heard a knock on my door. "Yeah?" I said, and both my moms came in.

That was my first sign that something was up. My

moms' usual motto is "Divide and conquer." As in, one mom per dealing-with-kid situation, whether it's me not finishing my homework or my sister playing her music too loud. Unless I'm in trouble. When that happens, I always get both moms.

"Hey, kiddo," said Jenny.

"What'd I do?" I asked, looking from mom to mom.

"Relax, you're cool," said Jenny.

"We just need to talk to you," said Karen.

"Okay," I said. "But I need to get over to Dash's house pretty soon."

"That's actually what we need to talk to you about," said Karen.

I glanced around. My room was kind of messy. They had probably come to say I couldn't go until I tidied it.

"Uh-huh," I said, trying to throw my room together before they could tell me to clean it. I yanked the pair of jeans under my desk chair closer to me. The chair teetered precariously, and Jenny reached out a hand to steady it, then lifted up one side of the chair so the jeans came free.

"Listen, Noah?" said Jenny. "Stacey called."

"We're not sleeping at Stacey's," I told her, balling up the jeans, then tossing them through the basketball hoop atop my hamper. "Swoosh! All net!" I added, palm out.

"Nice," said Jenny, delivering a high five. "She called to say that Dash can't have a sleepover tonight after all."

"What?" I couldn't believe Dash was bailing on me two weeks in a row. "I'm going to kill him! Why not?"

Jenny shot Karen a look but said nothing.

"Is it because he didn't finish his homework?" I asked. "I could help him get it done, honest. Can you call her back and ask?"

"It's not that, Noah," said Jenny. "It's about Gil."

"Gil? What about him?" Maybe Dash's dad was mad because we'd left the basement such a mess. Or maybe we got popcorn grease on his computer keyboard one too many times. Without waiting for an answer, I offered, "Well, then can Dash sleep over here? We haven't gotten to have a sleepover in, like, forever."

"Yeah, hon, that's not going to work tonight," said Karen.

"Noah, something happened," said Jenny. Her voice sounded tired and sad, like it did when she got laid off that time, even though Karen said she was better off without that stupid job.

Her voice made it sound less like a popcorn spill and more like a car crash. *Serious car crash?*

"Is Dash okay?" I asked.

"He is," said Jenny.

"Okay, good," I said, relieved but confused again. Karen started to cry, which surprised me, even though I've seen her cry lots of times. The weirder part was that Jenny looked like she was going to cry, too, and she never cries, ever.

"Then why can't we have a sleepover?" I asked.

"It's because of what happened with Gil, Noah. Stacey said he's not okay. That is, I mean, she said he—"

"Can I try?" Jenny interrupted, putting her hand on Karen's arm. "What we're trying to say, Noah, is something happened to Gil. We're not a hundred percent sure of all the details, because Stacey didn't elaborate. But we know it was bad. And the thing is, he didn't make it."

"'Didn't make it'? Like died?" I asked.

Jenny nodded solemnly.

"Died?" I repeated. "Like *dead*-died?"

I looked from Jenny to Karen.

"That's a joke, right? You're joking," I said. It had to be. This was Gil we were talking about. One of Dash's and my favorite scenes from *The Princess Bride* came to mind. It's the one where Billy Crystal, playing this super-old crackpot healer named Miracle Max, explains that Westley isn't actually dead. "There's a big difference between mostly dead and all dead," he says. "Now, mostly dead is slightly alive. Now, all dead, well, with all dead there's usually only one thing that you could do. . . . Go through his clothes and look for loose change."

We watched that movie with Gil a bunch of times. He'd quote it to us and we'd quote it to him. We'd done the sword-fighting scene with bananas, for crying out loud, only a couple of weeks earlier. There was no way the Gil I knew, jumping around the basement brandishing a banana sword, was dead. He couldn't even be mostly dead. The whole thing had to be a bad joke.

Or maybe something Dash made up as an excuse for bailing on our sleepover two weeks in a row.

"That's not funny," I told my moms.

"It's not a joke," said Jenny.

"Then it's a lie!" I yelled. Now that my volume was up, I couldn't turn it down, and it felt very important to pack up more sleepover things, even though I had already packed a bag. I ran around throwing stuff into it, like my clock radio and a random book or two and a stuffed animal I threw up on the day I won it at a carnival and still smelled like puke a little but was the only thing I ever won so I couldn't get rid of. I pulled my jeans out of the hamper and threw them in, too.

"We wish it were a lie, sweetie," said Karen. "I wish there were—"

"Stop saying that! Gil is fine! This is just Dash being a—a—dick!" I tugged on the zipper of my backpack, which was caught on my pajamas, and waited for my moms to react to me for using that word. I needed to get out of my room, out of my house, out of this stupid bad dream. "I'm going to go over there right now and tell him so."

Jenny grabbed me in a bear hug and I fought her, hard, howling and wailing the whole time. I'm sure Enid heard the whole thing, because she always hears everything that's happening in our house, even when her music is blaring. Seriously, she must be part bat—it's like she has sonar or something. But, thankfully, she didn't come in to investigate. I cried for a long time. I'm not even sure how long, but I remember Jenny on my bed and Karen in my chair next to the bed and feeling their hands resting on top of my blankets. I wasn't asleep, but my eyes were closed to shut out the world and everything in it. They must have thought I was asleep, though, because I heard them tiptoe out at a certain point. I opened my eyes and saw that it was dark out, and it crossed my mind that I never had dinner.

And that thought made me start to cry all over.

Dash's dad would never have another dinner. No Z-Burgers. No chili dogs or pepperoni pizza. No G-Force-grilled anything ever again.

I thought about going and climbing into the big bed, like I used to when I was little. I knew my moms wouldn't laugh at me or tell me I was too old for that. But I also knew seeing them would make it all real again.

So I lay there in the dark for a long time, unable to sleep and unable to think about anything but Dash's dad. How could this have happened? What kind of fatal accident could he possibly have had? All I could think of was Ben Franklin flying a kite in an electrical storm (I don't think he died?) and that Australian guy on the Internet who holds the world record for juggling chain saws while riding a unicycle—really dangerous don't-try-this-at-home stuff. Dash's dad wasn't like that. He was a comedy nerd like us. And pratfalls and *nyuk-nyuk-nyuk*s are supposed to be pretend. They're not even supposed to hurt, like Dash told Noa.

Dash. It suddenly occurred to me that he was probably in his bed thinking about all this, too. The night before, he'd had a dad. And now he didn't. Just like that. I wondered if Dash had gotten to see his dad one last time and say goodbye. Or if, like me, he hadn't known that the last time he saw him would be the last time. And so he hadn't said anything special at all. I tried to recall the last thing I said to Gil. It certainly wasn't "You're the coolest guy I know" or "I'll never forget you" or anything even close. I was pretty sure it was something unimportant like "I don't need a ride home." Or maybe even just "It's okay." Which felt ironic, because it was definitely *not* okay.

Once, when I went fishing on Long Island with my grandparents, my grandma Beth took a porgy that I'd caught and cut its head off on the dock and gutted it.

"Is it going to be okay?" I asked her afterward.

Enid was standing on the dock, too, watching the whole thing. "That," she said, pointing to the fish, "is pretty much the definition of not going to be okay."

Dash's dad was not a fish.

His house was nowhere near a dock.

This made no sense.

And I had a feeling it never would.

When I woke up Sunday morning, it was still mostly dark out. But the light in my closet was on, and there was this beam shining on my overnight bag on the floor.

It reminded me of how, when Dash and I were little, he was really bad at sleepovers and always decided to go home around midnight. His dad invented this thing he called sleepunders, which meant that Dash would bring pajamas and everything but he'd get picked up around nine-thirty at night and returned at about seven-thirty in the morning. We'd then watch cartoons and build with Legos and tape together cut-up paper towel tubes to make racetracks for our Matchbox cars and eat pancakes that Jenny would make when she eventually woke up. And it would be just like a sleepover except Dash got to be in his own bed for the sleeping part. It was genius. Dash's dad was genius.

Was?

That couldn't be right. Gil couldn't be a was.

The whole conversation with my moms the night before had to be a bad dream. Except if it was, I would've been in the bottom bunk at Dash's, or he would've been on the blow-up mattress next to my bed. No mattress, no Dash. Okay, fine, not a dream, but definitely some sort of mistake. Not a joke, exactly—Dash wouldn't prank me that hard—but a mix-up or something. Like the time I made breakfast in bed for my moms but forgot to use a coffee filter, so I ended up with brown sludge all over the counter and dripping into the silverware drawer.

Gil couldn't really be dead. Maybe I had misunderstood. Maybe what they meant was that he was really badly hurt, like so bad he *could* die. Life-threatening, but not necessarily life-ending. So he could pull through, like some superhero, against all odds. He might even have a nasty scar or amnesia, but he'd still be okay. He had to be okay. Right?

The house was quiet. So I did what I always do when I need answers. I tiptoed into the living room and clicked on the computer. But when I saw the cursor blinking at me on the search bar, I hesitated. What was I searching for, exactly? Answers, sure, but what was the question? I typed in:

"Is Dash's dad okay?"

I deleted it and tried again:

"Is 'mostly dead' really a thing?"

Delete.

"What could make people think you're dead when actually you're not?"

This time I hit return, but the results were so crazy I had to shut the search window. I felt frustrated and clueless, like some dumb little kid. According to my moms, when I was five or something, I proudly announced that I had googled them. They were confused until I showed them my search, which had two words in the search bar: "MY MOMS." Jenny actually took a screenshot of this and printed it out. It's probably still pinned to the bulletin board in her office.

This wasn't going to work. I needed real answers. So I went to the Happy Valley, which is what my moms call the charging dock we're supposed to leave our phones on at night (at nine, as if!). I unplugged my phone and texted Dash.

Me: Hey.
Me: U up?

No response. Maybe he was still asleep. While I waited, I went to the kitchen and poured myself a bowl of cereal. Finally, my phone lit up.

Maxx: Ye
Maxx: *yes

Quickly, I texted back.

Me: What happnd with yr dad? Is he OK?

The response came a moment later.

Maxx: No

No?

Me: What happnd?
Maxx: GTG
Me: Wait!

And then nothing. I tried again.

Me: Maxx?

More nothing.

I took my cereal bowl back to the computer, opened a new window, and watched a bunch of classic comedy clips on YouTube. After watching a few, I pulled up the *SNL* "Bass-O-Matic" sketch, but when Dan Aykroyd says, "Yes, fish eaters, the days of troublesome scaling, cutting, and gutting are over," I thought about the fish I'd caught and Dash's dad and what my moms had said and Dash's text. And I had to click out of it and go back to bed. I took my phone with me, but it stayed silent and dark. I thought about texting Dash again, but I didn't know what to say. I picked up the phone. Then put it down. Then picked it up. Scrolled through my messages. Put it down again.

Unable to figure out something smart to do, I did something stupid instead.

Me: Hey
Noa: Hi! What's up?
Me: Did u hear about dash?
Noa: Hear what?
Me: Dash's dad
Noa: What about him?

Oops. So, I guess she hadn't heard. I mean, why would she have heard? But now I had gone and told her, sort of. So she knew, but she didn't really know. And it was on me to tell her.

Noa: ????

I couldn't do it. What would I say? And what if it wasn't true? Sure, Dash had said that his dad wasn't okay, but that could mean a lot of things. I put the phone on vibrate, but as soon as I put it down, it started vibrating. Noa's name appeared, along with an image of a cow's butt that I'd assigned to her contact. I stuck the phone under my pillow, where it continued to vibrate. It finally stopped, only to start again a moment later. I peeked to see if it was Dash. Nope, just Noa calling back.

My bedroom door opened and a bright purple head of hair appeared. With raccoon eyes, just like Dash's dad.

"Answer your phone," Enid said sleepily before the door closed again. Only someone who's part bat could hear a vibrating phone from two rooms away with the doors closed. I obeyed, only to hear the voice I least wanted to hear.

"What about Dash's dad?" demanded Noa, like she hadn't just texted the exact same thing.

"I . . . uh, I don't really know," I admitted. "Something happened."

"Something like what?" she asked.

"Something bad," I told her.

"Like a car accident?" asked Noa. It surprised me that she went right there, not wasting any time on spilled popcorn or other less lethal hazards. Or venturing into electric-shock and chain-saw-juggling land.

"Maybe?" I said. "I don't really know. I thought you might know."

"Why would I know?"

"I don't know," I said again. "Just forget about it."

"How am I supposed to forget about it?" asked Noa.

"Look, maybe it's nothing," I said. "His mom told my moms something bad happened but they didn't get all the details."

"What does that mean?" asked Noa. "It's not, like, *serious,* is it?"

I didn't answer. I felt like I had said too much already.

"Noah!" She was clearly getting impatient with me. "What did his mom say? What were her words, exactly?"

"I have to go," I said. And then I hung up fast and put the phone in the back of my closet, behind the pile of sweaters Jenny washed in hot by mistake but can't be given away because Grandma Beth knit them.

That way, even Enid wouldn't hear if Noa called back again.

Chapter Five

"Go back up and change your pants," said Karen. She was standing near the door, wearing a black skirt and holding her keys. She sounded tired, even though I was the one who hadn't been sleeping. I'd gone into my moms' room several times the night before, and the night before that.

"What's wrong with my pants?" I asked.

"They're sweatpants."

"They're black," I pointed out.

"Change."

When I returned wearing my so-called temple pants, she looked at my exposed ankles and made a face.

"Wow. I guess maybe you have grown a bit."

"Really? You think?"

"Yup," she said. "Those are some serious high-waters. Tempted to make an ark joke."

"Thanks for resisting," I replied. Ask anyone named Noah and they'll tell you we get plenty of ark jokes.

We went out front and joined Jenny and Enid, who were waiting in Frau Blue Car. "I think we need to run an errand on the way. What time does Mr. Maxx open?" Karen asked them.

Enid pulled up the answer on her phone. "Ten."

Which is how I ended up with new temple pants. And why we ended up arriving at the funeral late and sliding in the back.

Yeah, *funeral.* Dash's dad's funeral.

It wasn't a joke.

Or a mistake.

Gil was gone.

I had never really imagined what my first funeral would be, but never in a million years would I have thought it'd be Dash's dad's. I mean, he was a dad, so he was old, but he wasn't old-old. I mean, Grandma Beth is much older. Dash's grandma is much older, too, obviously, which only dawned on me when I saw her at the funeral. This might sound dumb, but I had never thought about the fact that in addition to being Dash and Pete's dad, Gil was also someone's son.

I didn't really know what to expect. In movies, funerals sometimes have a dead guy lying there like he's asleep. Jenny and Karen reassured me ahead of time that this wouldn't be the case. They said there'd be a big, closed wooden box at the front of the sanctuary with flowers on top of it, and they were right. Rabbi Fred and Rabbi Jake and Phyllis were all there, and for the most part they ignored the box. I couldn't understand how they could just go about their business when all I could think the whole time was, *Gil is in that box, Gil is in that box, Gil is in that box.*

Rabbi Fred was in charge of the service. He likes to talk, and I'll admit that sometimes I tune him out when he's up there preaching on the bimah. But this time I paid close attention. The bizarre thing was, not only did Rabbi Fred ignore Gil's coffin, he barely talked about Gil at all. At least not the Gil I knew. He mentioned how Gil graduated at the top of his class in college and went on to be a journalist before going back to school for his law degree and becoming a successful trial lawyer on the partnership track at a big downtown law firm. He spoke of Gil's ambition and the pressure he put on himself to achieve, and he mentioned how many people admired him, which I'm sure was true. But he didn't talk about how funny Dash's dad was, or that he had done stand-up in college, or that he ran every morning, or that he loved seltzer and hot sauce and used his beloved G-Force grill for practically all of his cooking. If I hadn't seen Dash's mom and Dash's grandma and the back of Dash's head in between them, and a lot of the kids from Hebrew school, and even some of our elementary school teachers—including Mrs. Moseley, of all people—I might have thought I was at the wrong funeral.

I wished I was at the wrong funeral.

I wished I wasn't at any funeral at all.

I wished I could go back to when I last saw Gil. I wished I had gotten a ride home from him that Tuesday, even though Jenny would have been irritated when she came to pick me up and discovered I'd already left. It's so weird, seeing someone for the last time and not even knowing that you are. It made me think of the time I was racing my favorite Matchbox car and it rolled down the storm drain on our corner. My moms got me a new one, but it wasn't the same. I didn't want a new Trans Am. I wanted a do-over. I even think I asked God for a do-over and promised that I'd never ask for anything else in my whole entire life. It's hard to believe that I thought a dumb little toy car was worth giving up a lifetime of wishes.

Not that anyone ever really gets a do-over, I guess.

"Please rise for the mourners' kaddish," instructed Rabbi Fred. We all did, and Karen and I recited the Hebrew words to the prayer for the dead. I could hear Enid and Jenny tripping over the transliterated English version at the back of our prayer books.

"Yitgadal v'yitkadash shmay raba . . . ," we all droned together as one. Usually, since the kaddish is close to the end of a service, it's like a signal that there's only about ten minutes to go. The way our temple does kaddish is that before we do the prayer part, the rabbis read the names of anyone who has died recently or at this time of year in previous years. Anyone who is

related or was close to them stands up. Then the rabbis say that if anyone's name should have been on that list but for some reason wasn't called, their mourners should say the name and stand up, too. The rabbis also read a list of people who died due to violence in our city that week. And finally everybody who is able to stand is invited to join them, and when everyone is standing, we all say kaddish together. The rabbis explain that we do this because even if you're not mourning someone, you can offer your voice for those who have no one to say kaddish for them.

Gil's funeral was the first time I had ever stood up and done something other than saying the words and stretching my legs. It was the first time I stood in a room full of mourners as a mourner.

When we sat down after the kaddish, I felt inexplicably exhausted. It was like I had gone through some sort of time warp during the prayer and come out much, much older. Was this what old people went through all the time? Was saying "See you later" less of a reflex and more of a wish? No wonder some old people seem so grouchy. Grandma Beth isn't like that, though. It's true that when we talk on the phone, she always seems in a hurry to get off, but Karen says it's because in her day they charged for phone calls by the minute. Still, no matter how short the phone call is, she always says the same thing: "So far, so good!" Her other favorite saying is "Can't complain. Consider the alternative!"

Today was the first time I realized what she means

by "consider the alternative": *I could be dead.* No wonder she feels like she can't complain.

From there, my mind started to wander, almost as if it were doing its own kind of SND riff inside my head. "Consider the alternative" made me think of "pining for the fjords," which comes from that Monty Python sketch about a Norwegian blue parrot that's completely and obviously dead in its cage. In the sketch, Michael Palin keeps telling John Cleese that the parrot he sold him—they're clearly using a fake bird in the sketch—is not dead but just resting. "He's pining for the fjords!" he insists.

When Gil first showed us that sketch, he explained that "pining" means missing something you no longer have, and a fjord is sort of like a canal or a river. I pictured Gil standing on a bridge with a bright blue macaw on his shoulder like a pirate. The parrot, unlike the one in the Monty Python sketch, was a real one, very much alive. And so was Gil. He was smiling, albeit a little wistfully, almost as if he were pining for something. Like maybe to still be alive.

"Earth to Noah." A punch on the arm from Enid brought me back to the temple, which was close to empty at this point. "You planning on spending the day here?"

"What? No." I looked around, but everyone else seemed to have left the sanctuary. "Where's Dash?"

"Guessing he went to the cemetery," said Enid.

"Are we going, too?"

Enid shook her head. "Didn't you hear the rabbi? Immediate family only. They're having people back at Dash's mom's house later for shiva."

"But I'm Dash's best friend," I protested, even though I was actually sort of relieved. At Hebrew school, we had studied Jewish funeral practices, which include having everyone scoop a shovel of dirt onto the coffin. That hadn't struck me as problematic at the time. But then again, until Gil's funeral, I had never seen a real coffin, much less the coffin of someone I actually knew. Over the years, Dash and I had buried his dad in the sand at Bethany Beach lots of times. He was always a good sport about that, so maybe he wouldn't mind? But it still felt weird and disrespectful somehow.

Also, I've never really told anyone this, but I still hold my breath when I ride by cemeteries. That's because when I was little, Enid convinced me it was not polite to breathe while other people can't. I'm old enough to know it doesn't work that way, but for some reason I can't stop myself.

So when Enid said, "Sorry, Noah," I didn't argue about not going to the cemetery. Instead, we went home and made brownies while Karen made her famous triple-secret veggie lasagna from scratch (she adds tofu for extra protein and minced garlic for extra flavor . . . *shhhh!*). According to Karen, that's what we Jews do in times of trouble: we eat. I'm not so sure she's right, since Enid and Jenny are the same way and they're not Jewish, but I wasn't in the mood to argue with her.

It was a sad day, sadder than even a brownie-batter-covered bowl and mixing spoon plus a cat in your lap could fix.

When three o'clock rolled around, the food was done cooking and my moms finally said we could go over to Dash's mom's place. Enid stayed home, but she gave me an envelope to deliver. It was black and had a white dove painted on the outside. We let ourselves in when we got there, as directed by a little sign taped to the door, and I put Enid's card on top of a pile of other cards near the door. There were a lot of people there, some of whom I recognized from the service. My moms and I went over and hugged Stacey. Dash wasn't in the kitchen or living room, so I headed to his room.

"Hey," I said to Dash when I found him there. I was surprised to see that someone was with him already, and that it was Noa. She still had her coat on, so she must have just arrived, too. It was strange to see her at Dash's house. I almost forgot that we were both there for the same reason—because of what had happened to Gil.

"Hey," said Dash. He hadn't been at Hebrew school on Tuesday, or the Tuesday before, so I hadn't seen him in more than two weeks. The three of us stood there awkwardly.

"Cool tie," I finally said. "Wait, you've got something on it."

"Huh?" said Dash distractedly. He looked down, which was weird because usually he blocks me, then we Stooge it up with some fake eye gouges and stuff. But this time he didn't, so I had no choice but to finish the gag by knocking him in the nose with the finger I was using to point to the "stain." I winced a little, wishing I hadn't gone down this particular road, especially when Dash pulled back in surprise, then said, "Oh. Yeah, it was my dad's." He took the tie off and tossed it on a chair.

Noa gave Dash what seemed like a look of apology for my being an idiot. "I'm sorry about your dad," she said. As soon as Noa said it, I realized I had screwed up. Not just by pulling the dumb stain gag, but also by not offering my own "sorry" right away. I tried to fix things by piggybacking off hers.

"Yeah, I'm sorry, too," I said.

"Thanks," said Dash.

"It totally sucks," I added.

"Uh-huh," said Dash.

I stood there, not sure what to say next. I realized that since Dash and I hadn't really talked yet, he might not know that I didn't know how his dad died.

"So what happened?" I asked.

"Noah!" yelled Noa.

"What?" I said to her. "You were wondering, too." I turned back to Dash. "Was he in, like, a car accident?"

"Something like that," mumbled Dash.

That was a weird answer. I wanted to say, *Wait, was he or wasn't he?* But before I could open my mouth, Noa said to Dash, "People are going to ask you all sorts of stupid things. You don't have to answer them. You don't have to do anything you don't want to, actually." Then she glared at me.

"Thanks," said Dash. He sounded relieved.

I felt my insides go flop. I had no idea there were so many rules about what you should or shouldn't do or say in situations like this. I really wanted to say the right thing—something to make Dash feel better, not worse.

"Karen made lasagna," was what I came up with. Dash loves my mom's famous veggie lasagna.

"Oh," he said. "I haven't really been hungry."

"That's normal," said Noa, nodding sagely. "Still, you should try to eat something."

"I guess," said Dash.

"Maybe I could bring you some food?" I offered.

"I don't know. Sure." Dash seemed surprised by this idea, then pleased by it. "That'd be great."

"You got it," I said, jetting off to the dining room. I grabbed a plate and dug into my mom's lasagna, carving out a thick, meaty-yet-meatless rectangle (the third secret ingredient is portobello mushrooms), then another. I added four brownies to the plate. And three . . . okay, four rugelach. *There, that ought to do it.* I grabbed two forks, plus a cup of Dr Pepper for him and one for me, which I carried by biting the rim of the plastic cup. Jenny, who was standing in the arched doorway to the kitchen, glanced at me, took in my haul, and gave me one of those *Seriously?* looks. "For Dash," I informed her importantly through clenched teeth.

Dash's door was closed when I came back, and I had no free hand, so I kicked it to signal my return.

Noa opened the door.

"Thanks, Noah," she said. "That was really sweet of you."

She took the plate and the cup in my hand from me, continuing to stand in the doorway. Behind her, I could see Dash sitting on his bed with his laptop open. I shifted the cup in my mouth to my now-free hand and turned to slide by Noa, but she held up her palm and stopped me.

"Hey," she said quietly, in a just-between-us-friends voice. "Dash kind of wants to be by himself right now. Is that okay?"

"Uh, sure," I said. "I guess."

"Thanks," said Noa. "You're the best."

And then she closed the door. With her on the other side of it, in the room with Dash.

I knocked on the door. Noa opened it again.

"I thought you said Dash wanted to be by himself."

"Oh, yeah, he does," said Noa. "He just wanted to show me something first."

"Show you what?" I asked, wondering what Dash could possibly want to show her and not me.

"Noah, listen. Do you care about Dash?"

"Of course!"

"Great. The way to show him that is by respecting what he needs right now."

I opened my mouth, but before I could say anything, she shut the door in my face again.

I stood there, speechless. Of course I wanted to respect what he needed, absolutely. But why did he need for me not to be there? Was he mad at me for the stupid tie gag or something else I had done? I hoped that the plate of lasagna and desserts would show him that even my dumbest moves came from a good place.

Reluctantly, I shuffled back to the dining room, which is connected to the living room. I really wanted to get myself a plate of lasagna and desserts, but I also felt like throwing up. Dash's little brother and his friends were lying on the living room rug, watching some cartoon with gargoyles that transformed into robots, or vice versa. I sat down on the couch behind them and stared at the screen. The show was mindless in a good way, but since it was a show for six-year-olds, I started playing on my phone so no one could tell I was actually paying any attention to it. Pete seemed exactly the same as he had the last time I was over. Only a few days before, his dad was alive, and now his dad was gone and here he was, totally unaffected.

It must be nice being six. When I was six, I hadn't had anything truly bad happen to me, unless you counted dumb stuff like losing a toy car or getting my cubby stolen by Noa. I hadn't even met Dash yet. I couldn't remember who my best friend was before I met Dash.

The more I thought about it, the less I actually remembered about being six. Did this mean Pete wouldn't have any memories of this day? What if when he grew up, he didn't remember Gil at all? I looked at Pete, who was now sitting on top of one of his friends. I heard a fart noise, then Pete fell off his friend, laughing, and all the other six-year-olds tried to duplicate the effect by smashing their mouths on their forearms and blowing or sticking their hands in their armpits and pumping their arms.

"Gross," I said loudly, to make sure no one thought I was in on any of that. I got up and went to the kitchen to give my moms a pitiful look that said, *Can we go home now?* Noa's mom was patting Dash's mom's back and saying, "Don't beat yourself up, Stacey." The other moms all stood around, nodding sympathetically.

"I'm sorry," said Dash's mom. Just then, she noticed me standing there. She wiped her eyes quickly and wrapped me in a big hug. "Oh, Noah. Thank you for coming," she whispered. "It means a lot to Dashie. And all of us."

"Yeah, sure," I said. "I'm really sorry," I added.

Jenny and I walked to the car while Karen stayed behind to help Stacey. When we got in, Jenny let out a loud and long breath.

"I wish I could tell you that paying your respects gets easier as you get older," she said.

"It doesn't?"

"Nope. I mean, maybe once in a while, if the person is really old or has been sick for a long time. But this . . ."

Her voice trailed off and she turned on the radio. I guessed she meant because Gil wasn't really old or sick. Which made me think now might be an okay time to get some answers about Gil's death. So as she pulled out of the parking space, I asked, "Do you know what happened?"

"What, to Gil?" she asked.

"Yeah."

"Not entirely," said Jenny. "Stacey said a couple of cryptic things, but I don't really have the whole story."

"Cryptic?" I echoed. "Like what?" It sounded like the plot to a movie. Did Gil die under mysterious circumstances? Was he actually a double agent? I tried to imagine Gil sneaking around in a trench coat, carrying on his secret life.

Jenny didn't elaborate. Instead, she said, "Noah, I know this whole thing has been really upsetting—it has been for all of us. But you must have known Gil had some problems, right?"

"What kind of problems?" I asked, still picturing the movie version. Classified documents? A stolen formula? An elaborate cover-up? I saw Gil on the run, gasping for breath and looking over his shoulder while the bad guys closed in and—

Jenny stopped at a light and looked at me.

"I know you and Dash had a lot of fun with him. But the thing is, sometimes people work hard to keep up appearances. When inside they're really feeling—"

"Green," I said.

"What?"

I pointed to the light.

"Oh. Thanks." Jenny looked up and started to drive again, adding, "Look, we probably shouldn't jump to any conclusions. I'll talk to Stacey. If I learn more about what happened, I'll let you know. Okay?"

"Okay," I said.

Just then, we drove down Gil's block and went right by his house. It looked exactly the same as it always did. His car was even parked out front, so it looked like he was home. Maybe showering after a run. Or reading the paper, or working at his computer in the basement. Or cooking something with his G-Force grill. Or drinking a seltzer.

Except he wasn't doing any of those things. And he wouldn't ever again. I pictured Gil popping open a can of seltzer, taking a sip, and keeling over, poisoned. It suddenly occurred to me that maybe I didn't want to hear the gory details, if there were gory details. It's one thing if someone's telling you about a movie and they describe the blood and the guts and everything. It's another thing if it's not a movie. If it's real life and someone you know. Someone you care about.

We drove together in silence for a while, just listening to some kind of plinky jazz.

When we pulled up in front of our house and Jenny switched off the radio, I realized there was still one question I needed to ask.

"What about you?" I asked.

"What about me?"

"You're not going to . . . you know."

"What? Die?" asked Jenny.

I shrugged, embarrassed.

"I mean, eventually, yeah. But for the foreseeable future, you're stuck with us. In fact, our plan is to persecute you for as long as possible. Ideally while wearing matching sweatshirts that read I'M NOAH COHEN'S MOST EMBARRASSING MOM."

"Great," I said. Knowing my moms, she probably wasn't entirely kidding. A couple of days earlier, I would have called that a fate worse than death.

Now? Not so much.

Chapter Six

Dash didn't come back to Hebrew school the next Tuesday, or the Tuesday after that. I tried texting him a bunch of times, including to ask if he was mad at me and to apologize for whatever it was I'd done, but he never replied. Meanwhile, miraculously, while Dash was out—I feel kind of guilty about this—Hebrew school got a lot more fun.

Here's why: they started giving us seventh graders "team time" to work together on our mitzvah project. Some of the kids hadn't picked a comedian or joined a team, so the rest of us tried to suggest ideas for them. We started by making one list of all the Jewish comedy greats we could think of. Then people yelled out the names of other ones they thought might be Jewish, and Noa and I Jewgled them. (That's when you use a search engine to find out if someone is Jewish or not.) Rabbi Fred had given Rabbi Jake a printed list of his suggestions: Mel Brooks, Rob Reiner, Allan Sherman, and someone named Lenny Bruce, so we tried to decide which ones should go on our master list.

"Lenny . . . Bru . . . ," I repeated while copying the name into the search bar.

"Wait, guys, don't Jewgle him!" instructed Rabbi Jake.

"Ooo . . . ," said Maya, raising her eyebrows and elbowing me.

Rabbi Jake put a hand up to emphasize his point. "No Lenny Bruce, guys," he said. "Inappro-pro."

"Hey, speaking of which," asked Deena, "what about Amy Schumer? Or Sarah Silverman?"

"Yeah, there are hardly any women on the list," said Noa, sizing it up. "And no people of color, for that matter."

"Yes, there are," I argued. I live in a house full of girls (except Spud), so I am of course aware—and in favor—of the need to be inclusive in all things. "Right here." I pointed to the list. "See? We have Amy Schumer. And Gilda Radner. And Mayim Bialik. Tracee Ellis Ross from *Black-ish* is Jewish, too, I think. Plus Maya Rudolph. And Drake."

"Drake's a rapper, not a comedian," said Alex Weinberg.

"I beg to differ," I said. "He's hosted *SNL* on more than one occasion, including doing a digital short with

Andy Samberg. And did you see that skit he did about his bar mitzvah?"

I was gearing up to launch into my rendition of the sketch when I thought I heard Noa say, "And crusty."

"Drake's what?" I asked.

Noa smiled. "Not Drake. Krusty the Clown," she said. "You know, from *The Simpsons*? We should add him to the list."

I stared at her, surprised that such wisdom was coming from . . . *her*. She was right, of course. Krusty is definitely Jewish. His dad is a rabbi, and Krusty had a bar mitzvah and everything.

"Yeah, totally," I said. "I mean, unless we're only allowed to do real people."

"I think we should be able to use him," said Noa. "He's Jewish. He's funny. He's even a comedian."

We turned to the ultimate arbiter: Rabbi Jake.

He shrugged. "Sure, why not?"

I couldn't believe we were getting to spend Hebrew school time discussing *The Simpsons*. And then Rabbi Jake let me cue up a clip from the episode with Krusty's bar mitzvah. The only thing that made the experience less than perfect was the fact that Dash wasn't there.

Usually, Dash and I texted back and forth all the time. But now, when I texted, I got nothing in return. My moms suggested that I actually "pick up the phone and call him." To humor them, I gave it a try, but his voice mail wasn't set up, so I just hung up.

"Maybe he needs some space," Karen suggested. "Why don't you assume he's fine and just reach out to him every now and then to check on him?"

So I tried that. But no matter what I texted, the same thing happened. Or rather, didn't happen.

Me: Sup! It's me noaH (duh!)
Maxx:
Me: Yo. Txt me back u tool. The Israeli dance police r holding me hostage!!
Maxx:

Finally, in desperation, I tried something else.

Me: Where did u go? Take me wit u!!! Dying here . . .

Oops. Didn't mean to use the d-word. I quickly tried to fix things.

Me: Sorry!!! Didn't mean it like that!!!
Me: R u mad?
Me: If u want me to stop let me no.
Me: Just text something. Unless ur fone is ded.

Aaaaaand made things worse.

Me: Gah!!! Sorry again!!!

It was kind of nuts—no matter how chill I tried to make my texts, they came out the opposite. It was like at the shiva all over again. I kept saying the wrong thing, and every time I tried to make things better, I made them worse.

After that, I made a conscious effort to text him really boring questions like "What's up?" or "R u ok?" Still nothing. It got to the point where I began to get kind of worried about him. But when I called his house—that was also my moms' idea—Stacey said that Dash was fine and that she'd give him the message I called. Moms can forget stuff, though, so I'm not sure if he actually got that message, because I didn't hear back.

During one of our breaks between classes at Hebrew school, I went on my phone and checked Dash's social media accounts, which I did every couple of days. I was disappointed, but also relieved, to see that he hadn't posted anything recently.

"It's really for the best."

Noa's voice startled me into looking up. In a really condescending tone, she continued, "Dash staying off social media, I mean."

"Not that it's any of your business," I told her.

"Rude," said Noa, which was crazy because she was the one snooping over my shoulder. "I just mean that when you go through something like that, you need to protect yourself."

"Wow," I said sarcastically. "We're all so lucky to

have you here, since you're obviously an expert on everything."

"Not *everything,*" said Noa. "But what Dash is going through? Sure."

"Yeah, right," I said. "Because your dad is dead."

"Yes."

"Your dad is dead?" I repeated.

"Uh-huh."

"But I see him picking you up at temple every week."

"That's my stepfather," said Noa, looking at her fingernails and picking at a cuticle. "My dad died when I was little. He had pancreatic cancer."

"Oh," I said, feeling like an idiot. Then my shiva memory kicked in, so I added, "Sorry."

"Thanks," said Noa. "So, like I was saying, I can totally relate to what Dash is going through."

"I can, too," I told her. "I mean, I don't have a dad."

"Did he die?" asked Noa.

"No. It's just always been me and my moms."

"Okay, so you're aware that not having a dad in the first place isn't the same as losing one?" said Noa, her voice rising as she stood up.

"Yeah—I mean *no*! I just—" I didn't know how to explain it. I love my moms. They are the awesomest. With them, I have exactly no *need* for a dad. But *want* is different. I always felt like, if I had a dad, I'd want him to be like Gil. Yet I didn't see a way to explain that to her without making things even worse.

"Just forget it, Noah!" yelled Noa, causing everyone in the social hall to turn and stare at us. "Leave me alone, okay?"

And with that, she practically ran out of the room. Based on everything I've told you about Noa, you're probably thinking that was awesome, right? Getting her to move far away from me and not want to have anything to do with me has been my goal for my entire life, practically.

So why didn't it feel awesome? Possibly because my best friend was already not speaking to me. And then when my nemesis stopped speaking to me, too, I didn't have my best friend to tell about it!

For all these reasons, I was super-happy when Dash walked into Hebrew school a few Tuesdays later during skills class. He gave Rabbi Fred a nod, took his old seat, and slumped down in it. He didn't say a word, and when Rabbi Fred dismissed us for the break between classes, Dash practically, well, dashed on out of there.

I looked all over the building, but he was nowhere to be seen. I texted him again.

Me: Maxx! Welcome back! Wher r u?
Me: Helloo??

No response. And when I finally gave up looking, all the sign-ups for the good electives were already full, of course.

Which is how I ended up in Israeli dance again.

"If I didn't know better, Noah, I'd say you were becoming an Israeli dance fan," said Solly, the dance teacher, shaking a teasing finger at me. *"Mayim, mayim, mayim, mayim!"* he chanted along with the beat of the music, leading everyone toward the center of the circle. I clapped a beat too late, as everyone else was backing up. I could feel myself starting to sweat, so I signaled to Solly and jumped out of the circle for a water break.

"And the song claims another victim," joked Solly. He always says that because *mayim* is the Hebrew word for water.

I was in no rush to return to class, so I stood at the fountain, pressing the button and waiting for the water to get colder. Spacing out, I watched the water flow and flow. I released the button and it stopped abruptly. No hidden pipe. No unending circle of replenishment, unlike Rabbi Fred's water feature. The only thing that was unending was the stupid Mayim Mayim dance, so I went to the boys' room to kill some more time. "Killing time"—where did that expression come from? I imagined a clock tower, like Big Ben, bending over to rest its head on a guillotine block. That made me think of the dumb old Popsicle stick joke about the guy who threw a watch off a tall building to see time fly. When the watch hit the ground and broke into a million pieces, the guy would definitely have killed some time, but you'd never see *that* joke on a Popsicle stick.

Why did everything suddenly seem to be about death and dying? No matter what I did or said or thought, it was like the Grim Reaper was following me. I pictured him in his black hooded cloak, doing the grapevine step and waving his scythe at me.

Just then, I saw Dash coming out of the room we had been in for skills class. I ran over to him.

"Hey," I said excitedly. Dash was carrying his coat and backpack, so I asked, "You taking off? You just got here!"

"Yeah, I, uh, gotta be somewhere," he said vaguely.

"That's cool," I told him. "I'm just glad you're back. I was worried, I mean, since you weren't answering my texts and stuff. Not that you have to or anything," I added quickly.

"Oh," said Dash. "Yeah, I lost my phone last week."

Which didn't explain why he hadn't responded to my texts in many weeks, but I decided not to point that out. Instead, I said, "That sucks. You getting a new one?"

"I guess," said Dash.

"Well, if you get a new number, let me know what it is, okay?"

"Sure," said Dash.

"Cool," I said.

Noa came up to us. "Your mom's upstairs looking for you," she said to Dash.

"Okay, thanks," he replied. To me, he said, "Later."

"Later," I echoed, playing it cool. I put up my fist to bump, but he must not have seen it. I punched the air a couple of times so Noa wouldn't be able to tell I'd been left hanging.

As soon as Dash was gone, Noa turned to me.

"Aren't you supposed to be in Israeli dance right now?"

"Not that it's any of your business, but Solly gave me permission to step out," I told her. I invented a reason on the spot. "I need to grab my sweatshirt. I think I left it in skills class."

"Sure," she said, sounding unconvinced, so I ignored her and went into our skills classroom and pretended to look for it. Funnily enough, I had actually left it there (ha!), hanging on the back of my chair.

I was grabbing my sweatshirt, hoping enough time had passed that Israeli dance might be close to ending, when a flash of light caught my eye. I followed it to the floor and saw that it was a cell phone screen lighting up to announce a text message. I bent down to get it, fully intending to give the phone to Rabbi Jake or someone in the front office who could make an announcement.

When I picked it up, I realized that I knew whose phone it was. It was Dash's. I knew because of the case and also because I saw my final text—"Helloo??"—identified with our code name for each other: Maxx.

And then another text came in. It was from someone named CS. It contained one word exactly.

The word was, in fact, "Exactly!"

This single word told me several things all at once. Dash's phone was not lost. That is, he might have dropped it on the floor of the classroom, but he had it when he came to Hebrew school today. So he didn't lose it the week before, like he told me. Unless, I reasoned, the whole time he thought it was lost it was actually in his bag and then during class he somehow kicked or jostled his bag in such a way that it fell out on the floor without him realizing it.

Which raised several questions: If that was what had happened, his phone would definitely be dead, so how would it be receiving texts? And if that wasn't what had happened, why did he tell me he lost his phone? What possible reason would he have to lie to me about that?

Was it possible that Dash was actually sending texts to other people while ignoring my texts? Was he just ignoring *my* texts and lying to me about his phone being lost?

Why would he do that? I was his best friend!

Or was I? Who was CS?

As I stared at the phone, it dawned on me that I had several options. I could deliver it to Dash and wait to see what he'd do. But then he could just say thanks and pocket it and go back to acting weird, and I would have lost my chance to understand what was really going on. Or I could hold on to the phone to see what other texts came in, from CS or from others, and gather more evidence to use when I'd eventually return it to Dash and try to get some answers from him. All I'd have to do was wait for texts to arrive and read them on the lock screen, just like anyone else who had found the phone might do.

Or, instead of waiting, I could go into the phone and read all his texts.

Now, I know that last one sounds bad! But here's the thing. It was like I was holding a Magic 8 Ball in my hand, but not one with dumb, cryptic answers like REPLY HAZY, TRY AGAIN. This Magic 8 Ball had real answers to all the mysteries of my life, such as:

Why wasn't Dash speaking to me?

What was he saying to other people?

How might I get him to be my friend again?

I suddenly thought about that episode of *Seinfeld* where Jerry meets the guy with the fancy pen that writes upside down. The guy practically begs him to take it—"Take the pen! Take the pen! Take the pen!"—and Jerry hesitates and protests and finally, reluctantly, accepts it. The minute the guy leaves, Jerry's mom confronts him: "Whaddya take his pen for?"

It felt like that pen guy was in my head, badgering me like he did Jerry: "Take the phone! Take the phone! Take the phone!" It might sound crazy, but in that moment I felt like Jerry. I didn't want to take it, but I also felt like I had no choice. I desperately wanted to know what Dash was thinking and feeling so I could do a better job of helping him or even just knowing what to say. And since his head, along with his mouth, was closed, peeking inside his phone seemed like the next best thing. It occurred to me that maybe he even left the phone on the floor under his chair on purpose, hoping that I might find it. Sort of like a message in a bottle, only intended for one particular person: me.

I hesitated for a moment, finger out. Then I entered Dash's password—which, thankfully, he hadn't changed—and tapped the messages icon. It took me to a text conversation between Dash and CS.

The most recent text, like I said, was "Exactly!"

The one before that was from Dash. It read:

Dash: Or underwater or something.

The one before that was also from Dash:

Dash: Or like I'm numb or asleep

And the one before that was from CS:

CS: I know what you mean.

Before that:

Dash: It's like I'm not here. Or like a dream but not a good one

It was getting confusing reading the conversation backward, so I scrolled all the way to the beginning. The first text was from CS.

CS: Hey!

Dash: Hey.

CS: I just thought you might want to talk more. I mean text. You know.

Dash: Yeh. Thanx.

CS: You don't have to say anything.

Dash: U sound like dr. G.

CS: OMG. You see Dr. G? She's my therapist too.

Dash: I know. My mom got her from yr mom.

CS: LOL. Do you like her?

Dash: She's ok. I just don't feel like anyone gets what it's like.

CS: I know.

CS: I get it.

Dash: I no you do. Noah doesn't.

Dash: Like I no I'm not supos 2 but I kind of hate him now.

Wait—what?

It hadn't occurred to me that the texts might be about *me*. Here I thought I'd get a window into why Dash was acting so weird. Well, I got one all right. And, through that window, I could clearly see why Dash was avoiding me: he "kind of" hated me.

But why? I hadn't done anything! I mean, sure, I had read his texts, so maybe *now* he had a reason to be mad at me. But not when he wrote that text! Obviously, it was because of something that had happened before today. I scrolled back up and checked the dates. Sure enough, the conversation with CS started a few days after his dad died, on the day of the funeral.

The conversation went on and on. It jumped around a bit with "GTGs" and "TTYLs," but at least once a day it would pick up again. Every single day—including the week before, when he said his phone was lost—he had texted back and forth with CS.

CS. Who had those initials?

Chris Stern? That was the kid who thought skateboarding would be a good mitzvah project theme. He lived in Bethesda, too, I was pretty sure. Maybe he went to Dash's school? But Dash didn't hang out with him much, as far as I knew, though he did get a ride to Hebrew school with him sometimes. Chris Stern made sense because clearly CS knew who I was. After all, CS didn't say "Who's Noah?" when Dash mentioned me.

But why would Dash be texting with Chris Stern?

"Noah? Aren't you supposed to be in your elective?"

I jumped at the sound of a voice. Rabbi Fred was at the classroom door.

"Yeah, uh," I mumbled, wrapping my sweatshirt around Dash's phone to hide it and clutching the bundle to my stomach, "I gotta go. I don't feel so good."

I slid by him and bolted for the boys' room.

I locked myself in a stall and pulled out the phone again. Scrolling obsessively, I read and reread Dash's texts with CS. I checked out his other texts, too. There were also a whole bunch of unanswered ones, including mine and some from other guys from Hebrew school and regular school, plus quite a few from girls. I had no idea so many girls had Dash's number. I didn't see any from Noa, but she didn't strike me as one of those girls who do a lot of texting.

Dash didn't seem to be answering anyone's texts, except for his mom's and CS's. But most people just sent him one or two unanswered messages. "Sorry about yr dad" was a popular one, and a couple of the girls wrote "Thinking of u" with a bunch of emoticons, mostly little sad faces and flowers and stuff like that. My texts looked particularly pathetic all strung together and unanswered.

CS: Hey, you there?

I jumped when the new message came in. It hadn't occurred to me that Chris might not know that Dash's phone wasn't with Dash. I quickly ran through my options mentally. I could do nothing. If I ignored him, maybe Chris would stop texting. Or I could text back to let Chris know I'd found Dash's phone, recognized it, and would be returning it promptly to its rightful owner.

Or I could text back, pretending to be Dash.

Okay, once again, I think it's important to point out that I didn't mean to hurt anyone or mess anything up. Really!

CS: Want to come over after your therapy appointment?

Oh no. I had to say something, but what? Yes? No? Maybe? All options seemed destined to get me in trouble. But then I had a great idea. Instead of answering his question, I could try to get Chris to tell "me" (as Dash) why Dash was so mad at the real me (Noah). That way, I could understand what the problem was, apologize, and act like a better friend. And I promised myself I'd proceed carefully, making sure no one got hurt, and stopping as soon as I heard what I needed to know.

So I took a deep breath and tapped out a text:

Me [as Dash]: I'm just still so mad at him.
CS: Sure. I would be too.

Okay, good, we were getting somewhere. CS would also be mad, too . . . but he didn't say why. I decided to play dumb, figuring I could always backtrack if CS got suspicious.

Me [as Dash]: U wd 2 if what?
CS: You know. If my dad had.

Uh-oh. Chris was confused. He thought Dash was talking about being mad at his dad, not at me. I tried to address his confusion by acting confused back at him.

Me [as Dash]: Yr dad?
CS: Aren't you talking about your dad?

Good—confusion resolved. So I decided to try and clarify things.

Me [as Dash]: Not my dad. Noah.
CS: Why are you mad at Noah?

Now I wasn't just pretend-confused. I was actually confused. I typed quickly while trying to play it cool.

Me [as Dash]: Why do u think?

My hands started to feel slick with sweat as I anticipated the next text's arrival.

CS: I'm confused. Thought you were talking about what your dad did.

What Dash's dad did? What did that mean? Was Dash's dad a secret agent after all? Did he break the law? Or do something dangerous that got him killed?

I started to type a response, but just then, the bathroom door opened.

"Noah? Everything okay in there?"

The unmistakable sound of Phyllis's voice danced into the boys' bathroom.

"Gahhh!"

I'll admit it: I panicked. I stood up quickly, feeling a rush of embarrassment like my pants were down—even though they totally weren't. In my haste I lost my grip, and the next thing I knew—

KER-SPLASH!!!

Dash's phone stared up at me from the bottom of the toilet bowl.

"Augh!" I shrieked. Then, realizing how things sounded, I stammered, "I mean, I'm fine."

"Okay, no worries," said Phyllis. "Just take your time and come out when you're finished."

Great. I stared down at the phone and tried to figure out if reaching in and retrieving it would make things better or worse. I really wanted to just leave it there and wash my hands of the whole mess—literally. Except sooner or later, probably sooner, someone else would find it. And Phyllis would know that the person who had been lingering in that particular stall on the day in question was definitely me.

With my eyes closed, I reached into the icy cold, disgusting water and fished the phone out. I took it over to the sink, rinsed it off, wrapped it in paper towels, and shoved it in my sweatshirt pocket. I assumed it was dead, but it still seemed inconceivable to throw it away. My moms had made a big point of showing me exactly how much mine cost when they got it for me.

Now what?

I trudged back to Israeli dance.

Chapter Seven

That night, Enid showed up in my room.

"You know what I'm in the mood for?" she asked.

"To do my homework for me?"

"Vegan gingersnaps," continued Enid, ignoring my suggestion. "Wanna help?"

I considered. I was still feeling pretty lousy after the day I'd had. Cookies could definitely take the edge off. Even vegan ones.

"Okay," I said.

I followed her to the kitchen, carrying my algebra book in case our moms asked if my homework was done. Enid got out our moms' binder of recipes and started gathering ingredients, including molasses, brown sugar, flour, salt, cinnamon, and ginger. I saw her pull down the big glass jar of brown rice to get some-

thing behind it. And then I heard her go "Huh?" and I realized what had happened before I could stop her.

Enid being Enid, she got right to the point. "Why is there a phone in the rice jar?"

I didn't really have time to think. I just said the first thing that popped into my head, which was, "I don't know. It's not my phone. I have my phone." I held it out to show her.

Enid tilted her head to one side, so the long purple swoop of hair in the front slid down past her ear piercings. "Duh," she said. "I know it's not your phone. But it's cool. If you don't know anything about it, I'll just go ask the moms."

She turned to leave.

"Wait, don't!" I blurted out. Enid pivoted to face me. "You can't say anything," I begged.

"About what?" said Enid innocently.

Stalling for time, I turned my attention to creaming the vegetable shortening and sugar with the mixer. I hadn't planned on telling anyone what had happened. That was the best way to keep the world from knowing my secret—even I knew that. But then again, if anyone had to find out, it was probably best that it was Enid. It's not like she would tell my friends. Though she might tell our moms, unless I could convince her otherwise. When the mixture was so creamy I couldn't beat it any longer, I switched the mixer off.

"Sooo?" said Enid.

"It's Dash's phone," I said.

"What is Dash's phone doing in our brown-rice jar?"

"Trying to get more fiber in its diet?"

Enid didn't even crack a smile.

"Okay, fine," I said. "He left it at Hebrew school and I found it. I was going to give it back to him, except I, um, dropped it. I put it in the rice to dry it out."

Enid scooped some applesauce into the batter. It felt like she was plopping it in to make a point. "Dropped it?" she asked.

I turned away and stirred the bowl of dry ingredients, talking nonchalantly. "It was an accident. I was going to give it back but then Phyllis surprised me in the bathroom and it just—"

"Noah! You dropped Dash's phone in the toilet?!"

"I didn't mean to!"

"Why were you holding it over the bowl in the first place?"

"I wasn't holding it over the bowl. I mean, I was holding it, but I wasn't, like, dangling it. I was just—"

"And you put it in with our rice? Ewww!" Enid made a face. Then all of a sudden she said, "Wait a second, you were just *what*?" I stared at the floor and didn't answer. "Noah, tell me you weren't looking at Dash's private stuff on his phone."

"I didn't mean to," I said again. "I just . . . He got a text, and it popped up, you know, so anyone could see it. But the message didn't make any sense. So I wanted to make sure he was okay. That's all."

"So you just went into his phone and read his texts?"

I nodded, eyes closed and shoulders hunched as I awaited the lecture on violating someone's privacy that was clearly about to rain down on me. Which I totally deserved. Even for me, it was a pretty spectacular sequence of dumb decisions: picking up the phone, not returning it, reading the texts, and—worst of all—texting back as Dash.

Hearing nothing, I cautiously opened one eye. Surprisingly clear skies: Enid had added the dry ingredients to the wet ones and was mixing thoughtfully. Next she pulled out two cookie sheets, lined them with parchment paper, and began rolling pieces of the dough between her hands until they turned into little balls.

"So, what did you see?" she finally asked.

"You have to promise not to get mad," I said. "Seriously, I'm not going to tell you anything else unless you do."

"I promise," said Enid.

"No crossed anything?"

Enid held up both hands as proof. One at a time, because she was holding a ball of cookie dough. I rolled up my sleeves, reached into the batter, and joined her.

"I saw some texts that were between Dash and this kid we go to Hebrew school with, Chris Stern. I guess he and Dash are friends now or something. Dash told Chris he was mad at me. And Chris said he would be, too, because of what I did. But that didn't make any sense, because I didn't do anything! And when I asked what he meant, Chris said he wasn't talking about *me,* he was talking about his dad—that is, Dash's dad. And then—"

"Wait a second, Noah. You *answered* his texts? You texted back pretending you were Dash?"

"I, uh, not exactly," I said, backpedaling. "I mean, I never said either way. I just—"

"Noah!!" Aha, here was the storm. "I can't believe you! This goes way beyond violating someone's privacy!"

"I had no choice! Dash wasn't talking to me. So I had no idea what he was thinking or feeling."

"Oh, so that makes it okay?"

"No. I mean . . ." I looked down and the vegan cookie dough caught my eye. "Let's say you had a list in your pocket of everything you eat and don't eat. If someone was making you lunch and they couldn't read that list, they'd have to guess and they might serve you something totally offensive to you. Like a tuna melt or a meatball sub! But if there was some way for them to peek at that list, it would help you get a lunch you could actually eat and save a lot of innocent animals' lives! Wouldn't that make it okay?"

Enid raised an eyebrow. "That is the stupidest analogy I've ever heard. Animals were not going to end up as lunch if you didn't break into your friend's phone and read his texts."

"You don't know that," I said weakly.

"Noah! Jeez! Get the sugar."

I did as I was told, and she poured out a generous quantity into a shallow bowl. I joined her in taking the cookie dough balls we'd made and rolling them in the sugar until they were fully coated, then lining them up in rows on the cookie sheets.

"Go back to the part about what you read," she ordered. "What else did this Chris kid say about Dash's dad?"

"He said he'd be mad, too, if his dad did what Dash's dad did."

"And then what?"

"And then nothing," I told her. "That's when I dropped the phone. It didn't work after that, so I couldn't ask anything else. I mean, even if I wanted to."

"You don't want to know?"

"Know what?"

"What happened to Gil," she said.

"I mean, of course I want to know. But it seems like no one really knows the whole story," I informed her, adding more dough balls to the bowl of sugar. "I asked Jenny after the shiva, and she said Stacey was 'cryptic' about the details. She said she'd tell me if she found out more, but she hasn't."

"I know," said Enid softly.

I froze. "What do you mean, *you know*?"

"I mean, I heard our moms talking. But I already kind of suspected. They just confirmed it."

"Confirmed what?" I saw her hesitate, so I grabbed her arm. "E, come on, you've got to tell me. He was a spy, right?"

"A what?"

"I dunno." I felt embarrassed. "I just thought—"

"Look, Noah. Gil had a lot of problems."

"Why does everyone keep saying that?"

"Because he did. And I guess they must have gotten to be too much for him."

"So?"

"So Gil committed suicide," said Enid.

I felt like I had been punched in the throat. I shook my head slowly from side to side, unable to breathe or swallow. I didn't say it, but the word echoed throughout my head. I put my hands over my ears as if that could block it out or take it back.

"No," I said, my breath rushing back like I had just run the hundred-yard dash in PE. "There's no way Gil killed himself!"

"He did, Noah. I'm sorry."

"No, he didn't! You must have heard wrong."

Enid didn't say anything, but we both knew that was impossible. Her hearing capabilities are the stuff of legend.

"Gil would never do that, no way," I insisted. I stormed around the kitchen, unable to sit still any longer.

"Okay. So what do you think happened?"

I didn't want to tell her about the spy movie scenarios I'd been playing out in my head. They suddenly seemed as ridiculous as what she was suggesting. So instead I said, "I don't know. He was old. Old people just drop dead sometimes. You know, of heart attacks and old age. Or, what do they call it? Natural causes!"

"Natural causes?" said Enid. "Gil was what? Forty-five years old, maybe? Super-fit, out there jogging every day. Mental health–wise, though, different story."

"But what about Dash? And Pete! There's no way he'd do that to them."

"Probably he couldn't see any other option. Maybe he even thought it was best for them. I mean, obviously, if he'd been thinking clearly, he wouldn't have shot himself."

"Shot?! With a *gun*?"

"Noah, I'm so sorry," she said. She put her arm around my shoulders and sighed. "I probably shouldn't have said anything."

I started to cry, so I bit my lip hard to keep the tears from falling and squeezed my eyes shut to keep everything dark.

"Jenny promised!" I wailed angrily. "She said if she found out anything, she'd tell me."

My heart and my head were pounding. I pictured Gil on the basement floor, crawling toward the stairs, trying to call 911. He was lying in a puddle that definitely wasn't Dr Pepper.

But why would he call 911? And what would he tell them?

I've been shot.

And when the 911 operator asked, *Who shot you?* what would he say?

Me?

Then something else occurred to me. I looked up and asked Enid, "Does Dash know?"

"Probably," she said. "I mean, you said this Chris kid was texting with him about what his dad did, right?"

"Wait a second, *Chris* knows, too?"

"Not necessarily," she said, but I could tell she was just trying to be nice. "I mean, it sounds like it," she admitted. "But maybe you should talk to Dash."

I snorted to show her what I thought of that idea.

I wasn't sure who I was madder at: Jenny, for lying to me and treating me like a little kid. Or Dash, for telling his deepest, darkest secrets to Chris instead of me. It felt like the whole world was pushing me away, keeping me in the dark, locking me out. It felt lonely and awful, like no one thought I was important enough to talk to.

Including Gil. He never said anything about having problems. And he didn't say goodbye. At least, not to me.

It wasn't until the first batch of cookies came out that Enid and I realized something. She bit into one first and made a face.

"What?"

"Cookies are a little, uh, salty?" she said.

I picked up one and took a bite. "Bleahhh! What the—"

Enid licked a finger, then dipped it into the bowl

of sugar we'd rolled the cookies in. She touched her tongue and winced.

"I guess we weren't paying attention," she said. "We must have rolled them in salt, not sugar."

"You've got to be kidding me," I said. For years we've joked about this, since our moms keep all our kitchen staples in these big identical glass jars. The salt one has a blue lid and the sugar one has a green lid, so on April Fools' Day my classic move is always to switch the lids. "I guess I can't do anything right these days."

"They're not so bad. Maybe Spud would like them?" Enid suggested. "He likes salt licks, right?"

"Yeah, but he can't eat all of them. They'll make him sick." Just then, Jenny came into the kitchen.

"I smell cookies!" she sang out, reaching for one. Mid-bite, she stopped, her face frozen.

"What's wrong?" I dared her.

"Nothing," she said with her mouth full, chewing and trying to choke it down. "Interesting. Maybe a little . . . um, salty?" Jenny put down the half-eaten cookie and began to fill a glass at the sink.

"I dunno," said Enid, biting into another one. "I think they're an acquired taste. I mean, they're weird, but I can't stop eating them." She shot me a look that clearly meant *Talk to her,* then took a handful, wrapped them in some paper napkins, and slunk back to her room.

"Yeah, we accidentally rolled them in salt instead of sugar. Sorry. Guess I forgot to tell you," I said pointedly.

Jenny looked at me suspiciously. "Is something wrong, Noah?" she asked.

"Wrong? Why would anything be wrong?"

"I don't know. You sound angry."

"Why, because I ruined the cookies?" I tried to laugh like a bad guy in the movies. "Who cares? Besides, it's not like I did it on purpose," I added.

"I didn't say you did," said Jenny.

"Yeah, well, I didn't say you did," I said.

Jenny tilted her head to the side. "What are you talking about, Noah?"

"Nothing!" I got up and went to leave the kitchen. Over my shoulder, I said, "It's just, sometimes people say they're going to do something, and then they don't. And they act like it's no big deal. Even though it is a big deal."

"Noah, come back here. Sit down."

Reluctantly, I trudged back into the kitchen. I didn't want to have to look at her, so I grabbed my algebra book off the counter and pretended to study the problems instead. If Marvin had ten apples and Sam had half as many as Kayla and Kayla had five times as many as Marvin, they all still had things pretty good. You didn't see any of them committing suicide.

"Is this about Dash?" asked Jenny.

"No! It's about you being a liar!" I spit the words at her.

Jenny stared at me with a strange look on her face.

"Noah, in this family we don't call each other names—" she started to say.

But I couldn't listen, I was so mad. I cut her off, saying, "Oh yeah? Well, in this family we don't lie to each other!"

"What are you talking about?"

"You told me you didn't know how Gil died. And you said if you found out more, you would tell me. But you didn't tell me. And you *did* find out more. You found out he killed himself. Didn't you?"

Jenny's eyes got wide. "Noah—"

"What?!"

"Ohhhhh—" Jenny put her hands over her face and let all her breath out at once. "It's complicated, okay?" She slid her palms down her face and peered at me over the tips of her fingers. "You have to understand that when I said that, I meant it. I had every intention of telling you the truth, really. But then, when Stacey shared more information with us—well, we were pretty shaken up."

"So you just decided to say nothing?"

"Of course not, Noah. It's not like we made a plan or tried to deceive you. It's just, we weren't sure what to say or how to say it."

"You could say he blew his brains out."

"Noah!" Jenny sounded shocked. "Where did you hear that?"

"It doesn't matter where I heard it. Did he?"

Jenny was silent for a moment. Then she said, "Yes. Gil shot himself."

I heard a small gurgling noise and realized it had come from me.

"I am so sorry, Noah," Jenny continued. "I just— The whole thing was so overwhelming. And, honestly, we were pretty horrified, too. We had no idea he had a gun! I mean, all those nights you slept over there, and we didn't have a clue."

She picked up another cookie and started tapping it against the plate to shake the salt off. But the salt, for the most part, wasn't coming off.

"Maybe it was an accident," I suggested. "I mean, don't people with guns have accidents sometimes?"

"That's what I asked Stacey," said Jenny. "She said it wasn't."

"But she wasn't there, right? So maybe—"

"I know it's hard to fathom, but Gil wanted to end his life. He'd tried before. Not with a gun, but with pills."

I stared at her, wondering what could possibly make someone want to "try" something as awful, and as final, as that. "Try" didn't even seem like the right word for something like that. You could try all sorts of things for all sorts of reasons, like to get into the *Guinness World Records* book or win a million dollars. Or just to be able to tell your friends you tried a vomit-flavored jelly bean. Because even if it made you sick, you'd be okay.

Gil was not okay. Gil would never be okay again.

"It doesn't make any sense," I said.

"It doesn't," she agreed.

"He wouldn't leave Dash and Pete. Or me."

"I know. He was our friend, too," said Jenny.

"Mom?"

"Yeah."

"My stomach hurts."

"Oof, me too," said Jenny. "Too many salty cookies," she added, even though we both knew that wasn't why.

That night, Enid was out, so my moms suggested I pick a movie for the three of us to watch. Usually, I jump at the chance to make them watch Woody Allen classics (or the occasional Will Ferrell movie), but for some reason I decided to go for an old favorite from way, way back: *Aladdin.* I'm not sure why, but getting away to a "whole new world" filled with flying carpets and magic lamps had an irresistible appeal. I got a little sad listening to how Aladdin had the most perfect, awesome friend ever in the genie, but other than that, it did the trick. When the movie ended, I closed my eyes and lay there, motionless, like I used to when I was little.

"You think we should wake him?" I heard Karen ask.

"Nah. Poor kid, let's let him sleep."

"Okay," said Karen. "Shhh. C'mon."

I felt my moms slip out from beside me on the couch and pull the crocheted afghan up over my shoulders. A few minutes later, a heavy, warm thing settled into the spot behind my knees. But even with Raspberry purring like a lawn mower, I couldn't sleep. I thought about how much I loved running around with a bath towel on my head when I got out of the tub, pretending I was Aladdin. That was such a long time ago, before I even met Dash. I suddenly remembered that Robin Williams, who voiced the genie, also committed suicide. Robin Williams seemed a lot like Gil—playful, funny, and game for anything.

Was it a funny-guy thing? How could that be? Suicide was the most unfunny thing I could think of. Although I had seen lots of comedy bits about suicide over the years. Like in the classic bit where Fanny Brice plays a wife who wins the lottery, then finds out her husband gave away the winning ticket. "You should drop dead," she says. "I'll jump out the window," he offers. "Who stops you?" she yells back at him. And in *Hannah and Her Sisters,* Woody Allen tries to kill himself with a rifle. The gun goes off, but the shot misses him completely. So Woody goes out to see a Marx Brothers movie that ends up cheering him up and giving him a new appreciation for life.

Cheering him up. I thought back to that night of SND, which ended up being the last time the three of us would ever play it together. Would Gil still be here if we had gone upstairs and refused to do SND without him? Or if we had shown more appreciation for the old comedy clips he loved instead of always making him watch stuff like Miranda Sings with her smeared lipstick or Keith Apicary beating himself up in his underwear? "Chopper 4," for crying out loud—why did we make him watch it again and again?

I'm sorry, Gil, I told him silently. *I'm so sorry.*

What I wouldn't give for one more SND, a do-over round. Only this time we'd do everything right. We wouldn't tease him about his monkey arms, or spill Dr Pepper on his floor, or make him rewatch the same dumb videos. And when he went upstairs to "take a break," we'd go get him and bring him back down and let him pick all his favorite videos to watch. And we'd give him a million points so for once he could win instead of us. Who cared about being undefeated? What did it matter, if we could never play with him again?

When I finally fell asleep, I dreamed that I was flying the Chopper 4 helicopter. Down below, Gil was in a raging river, struggling to keep from drowning. I kept swooping in to lower a rope to save him, and I missed, again and again and again. His head kept slipping below the churning water, so when I woke up, the first thought I had was: *I have to go back to sleep because, if I hurry, I can get there in time.*

Chapter Eight

The next Tuesday afternoon, Noa and I both had to stay after school to make up a French quiz. So when we finally got on the bus, it was obvious that all the other Hebrew school kids had taken the earlier one. With my usual audience not there, I decided to skip the stand-up and actually sit for once. Noa was across the aisle from me, so I leaned over to discuss important matters.

"Have you watched any more Stooges clips? I've narrowed down my top ten. We could maybe highlight—"

Noa cut me off. "I feel like we should hold off on making any decisions without Dash. I mean, the last thing I'd want is for him to think we're leaving him out."

"Oh. Yeah. I mean, me too," I said.

"For all we know, he doesn't even want to do this anymore."

"Why wouldn't he?"

"I don't know. Maybe he's not in a comedy mood? You know, because of his dad."

That honestly hadn't occurred to me.

"Did he say that?" I asked.

"No," said Noa. "At least, not to me. Has he said anything to you?"

"No," I admitted. "I mean, we really haven't talked much at all since . . . everything."

"Okay, well, I'll ask him," said Noa. "But in the meantime, I have something cool to show you."

She reached into her backpack and pulled out a thick three-ring binder. Inside was this chart she had made, which she told me was called a spreadsheet. It was printed in about ten colors of ink, one for each category. The binder had rainbow-colored tabs and a big rainbow and unicorn sticker on the cover.

"Where's the cool thing?" I asked.

Noa rolled her eyes. "Duh. My spreadsheet!" she said proudly. "I'm kind of a whiz at Excel."

The chart—sorry, *spreadsheet*—turned out to be a list of all the different parts of our b'nei mitzvah service. She walked me through it and pointed out the parts she had already divided up—the various aliyahs, prayers, and other responsibilities. "These are the ones I'll do, and here are the ones I thought you'd want to do. Don't worry," she added. "I gave you the easier parts."

Despite the fact that Noa's binder and chart had orange and yellow and all the other colors of the rainbow, the only one I saw was red. It felt like she was bragging that she'd do a better job with the harder parts. Which might be true, but I didn't like her deciding it without even discussing it with me. I just let her rattle on and on, tuning her out. But then I noticed she had put the chart away and was pointing at the unicorn on the front of her binder.

"Don't you think that would be perfect?"

"What would be perfect?" I asked.

Noa made a really exasperated noise and pointed again to the sticker. "Like I *just said,* for our b'nei mitzvah, we could use a rainbow as our symbol. We could put a rainbow on the program and talk about it in our speech and everything. I mean, you know, kind of perfect because of our names. Also, as a gesture of support to Dash for what he's been going through."

"I don't think he'd want that," I said.

"Why do you say that?" asked Noa, looking worried.

"I dunno," I said. "It just doesn't sound like something he'd like."

The bus jerked to a stop across from temple, so I stood up quickly and got off. I felt weird, even though I hadn't lied to Noa. It *didn't* sound like something Dash would like. I remembered the first Tuesday after Gil's death, when Rabbi Fred gathered the entire seventh grade together and shared the news of what he called a "tragic and untimely loss." We all made condolence cards for Dash and put them in a manila envelope, then we all signed the envelope. It was probably still sitting at his house, unopened. Dash hated having people feel sorry for him. Like when he broke his leg in fourth grade, he let everyone play with his crutches, but he wouldn't let anyone—not even me—carry his backpack.

But what I didn't say, at least not then, was that it also didn't sound like something *I'd* like. The last thing I wanted was to call attention to the two of us having the same-sounding name, and that name being Noah, like Noah's Ark. Cue the ark jokes, people!

In skills class, I discovered that Dash wasn't there again. So much for talking to him. I pulled out my phone to send him a text, then remembered that he couldn't get it because I still had his phone. Thankfully, Noa had to step out for bat mitzvah tutoring with Rabbi Fred, but I could tell she wasn't going to let the whole rainbow thing drop. I could already picture what she was hoping for: a whole rainbow-themed b'nei mitzvah. Complete with a rainbow dress for her, a rainbow suit for me, matching rainbow tallises, a DJ spinning songs like "The Rainbow Connection," and giant rainbow lollipops on every table (okay, that part sounded good, but that wasn't the point!). And to make matters worse, she was trying to guilt me into doing it by saying it was for Dash.

Sure enough, as soon as we went downstairs for the break, I found out that Noa and I were both assigned to sell snacks, so there was really no escaping her. I was snack stocker, she was on money, and we were stuck sitting together at the snack table while kids streamed past us, shoving singles at us and grabbing at our limited selection of popcorn and fruit rolls.

"It's not because of your moms," she whispered.

"What?"

"The rainbow thing. I mean, rainbows are a great symbol for equal rights and lots of things, but that's not why I chose them. Hey! No money, no snack!" she yelled at a sixth grader, who made a face at her, grabbed a bag of popcorn, and ran off.

"Okay, I get it," I said. "But I still don't want to do it."

Noa's eyes followed the sixth grader across the room. She looked tempted to chase him down, but she stayed seated. Unfortunately, she was unwilling to let me off the hook so easily.

"Why not?" she demanded.

"In case you've forgotten," I responded, "it's my bar mitzvah, too. Or am I not allowed to have any opinions?"

"Of course you are, Noah. It's just . . ." She sighed, straightening the pile of dollars. "Look, this isn't about us, okay? It's really for Dash. I feel like with all he's been through, we should show him that he's not alone. That's what Dash needs right now."

"Who died and made you the authority on what Dash needs?" I asked.

"What's *that* supposed to mean?" asked Noa.

"I dunno. What if you're wrong?"

Noa was silent for a moment. We watched some fifth graders getting into a duel with the paper strips that come with the fruit rolls. Rabbi Jake seemed to be having little success getting them to stop.

"I'm not wrong," she finally said. "Trust me, I know what it's like to lose someone like that."

There she went again, acting like she was the grown-up and I was just a stupid little kid who didn't know what was what. It made me so mad. So instead of keeping my mouth shut like I should have, I decided to give it right back to her.

"Yeah, sure," I said.

"I do," she said before turning her back on me to take the dollar from the next kid in line.

"*You do* think you know everything. *You do* think you have some kind of special magic rainbow connection to Dash. But you know what? *You don't* actually know everything about what he's going through. Unless *your* dad killed himself."

Noa spun around, her mouth open like a fish. "What did Dash tell you about his dad?" she demanded.

"Nothing," I said, trying to sound nonchalant but feeling anything but. It was actually true, of course, though I hoped she wouldn't call me out on it.

Without warning, she bolted from the snack table, knocking the cash box over in her haste. Dollar bills went flying everywhere, attracting the attention of the sword-fighting kids, who ran to grab handfuls of money and make it rain again. Through the chaos I saw Noa heading into the girls' room. Sarah, Deena, and some of the other girls followed her in, glaring at me over their shoulders.

"Are you going to take my money?" asked a freckle-faced kid who had materialized in front of me. He was thrusting a handful of bills from the floor in my direction and casting a greedy gaze at the snacks. A bunch of other kids were now picking up the scattered money under the stern glare of Rabbi Jake. I kicked the would-be looter out of the snack area and was attempting to recount the money when Rabbi Fred came over.

"Everything okay?" he asked.

"No problem," I told him. Because what else could I say? Noa was still in the girls' room. But I could tell that when she came out, my problems were going to get a lot worse.

It's never a good sign when you'd rather stay in Israeli dance class than get pulled out. When Rabbi Fred showed up and crooked a finger for me to join him, I pretended not to notice and kept right on grapevine-stepping until Solly turned off the music and told me to go. We went to the library, thankfully. Rabbi Fred's water feature was more than I could take in my current condition.

I figured Rabbi Fred must have spoken to Noa, so I was not surprised to be pulled out of class. I was expecting him to say something like "Can you tell me why Noa got so upset?" Or maybe "Can you explain why you were so insensitive about Noa's father's death?" Or perhaps "Can you help me understand why you needed to prove to Noa that she doesn't know everything about what Dash is going through?"

He said: "How does getting some fresh air sound to you?"

Now that surprised me.

"Right now? Sure. What for?" I asked. We never get to go outside during Hebrew school, unless it's for an activity like sukkah decorating or getting on a bus for a field trip.

"Change of scenery. Stretch of legs. Unless you'd rather get all your exercise in dance class?"

"No! That sounds great. But can we just, like, do that?"

Rabbi Fred shrugged. "I'm the rabbi. Who's gonna stop me?"

I couldn't argue with that, so I waited while he got his coat and told the front office people he'd be stepping out with me "for a few." I had a pang of jealousy, wondering if Rabbi Fred did this with other students on a regular basis. Of course, it also occurred to me that maybe he only took walks with kids who caused trouble.

Andrea, the security guard who monitors the front door every Tuesday afternoon, gave us a nod like our leaving the building during Hebrew school was no big deal. Together we walked out of the synagogue and down the front steps. Rabbi Fred led the way, turning right on Wisconsin, then left, then heading straight for a while. He didn't say much, which was unusual for him. I didn't ask him where we were going because his stride suggested he had a destination in mind. Sure enough, after we walked down a hill, he said, "This way," and I noticed a small brown trail marker.

One of the coolest things about Washington, D.C., that not everybody knows is that in addition to Rock Creek Park, which is like a big forest that happens to be located in a city, there are also these cool trails that connect to stuff, like the zoo and the C&O Canal. When I was little, my moms used to take me and Enid hiking on the weekends, so I've been on a lot of the trails. Though I have to admit that a lot of them look the same, so I'm never a hundred percent sure if I've been on any of them before unless there's a really obvious landmark, like this old mill on a trail near the zoo, or this bridge that's on a trail behind my favorite playground.

So when Rabbi Fred asked, "Is this trail familiar to you?" my answer was, "I think so." But when we walked down the trail a little bit, we crossed a creek and I had a vague memory of standing in the rain holding a bag of stale bread. At first I thought maybe I was confusing this spot with another one where my moms used to take me to feed the ducks, but I asked anyway.

"Did we do tashlich here?"

Rabbi Fred smiled. "I wondered if you'd remember that. Yes, we did, once, a long time ago, before our congregation grew and we needed to find a more spacious, if less convenient, location."

"Was it raining?" I asked.

"It was pouring, as I recall. And, if memory serves, there was a dog—"

"Yes!" It all came rushing back to me. We had done community tashlich in this spot, all of us crowded on the banks of this tiny creek to cast our "sins"—in the form of bread—into the water, like we do every year to get ready for Yom Kippur. And then out of nowhere, a huge dog appeared and grabbed several of our bread bags and wolfed them down. "He even ate the bags!"

"I can only imagine how sick that dog became. Eating all that plastic."

"Eating all those sins!" I said. We both laughed, then fell silent. I suddenly remembered why we were here.

"I'm sorry," I told Rabbi Fred. "I mean, about Noa. I dunno why I did that. She just kind of pushes my buttons."

"So I've observed," said Rabbi Fred.

It made me feel guilty that he was being so nice, so I offered, "I guess I probably push hers, too."

"You might say that."

"I mean, I know I should probably apologize. But she should, too."

"Oh?"

"Yeah. For acting like she knows everything. Especially when it's about my best friend."

"You're talking about Dash?"

"Uh-huh," I said. I picked up a little stick, studied it, then threw it in the water and watched it slowly drift away.

I was tempted to tell him the whole story, but before I could launch into it, Rabbi Fred asked, "You haven't by any chance seen his cell phone, have you?"

His question caught me by surprise. My heart started to pound in my chest and I felt myself starting to sweat, and not just because of our walk.

"No. Why?" I said.

"His mother called and said he misplaced it recently. She thought maybe he had left it at Hebrew school last week. I'm sure it'll turn up, but if you happen to see it, can you let me know?"

"Sure," I said. "I'll keep an eye out for it." Look, I know lying is bad. And lying to a rabbi takes it to a new level of badness. I'm not sure what happened. My mouth just sort of took over for my brain. But once I said it, I couldn't take it back. *It's okay,* I told myself. *You'll give the phone back, and no one will have to know. Except for Enid. And God.*

Next tashlich, I was going to need a lot of bread.

Just then, another stick landed in the river. It followed the path of mine. I picked up another one, and so did Rabbi Fred.

"Care to race?" asked Rabbi Fred.

"Sure," I said.

"I should probably warn you," said Rabbi Fred. "I was the stick-racing champion of my yeshiva."

Together we walked down the trail to a little bridge we'd spotted. Standing in the middle, facing upstream, we held our sticks steady and, on the count of three, dropped them into the water. The bridge was narrow enough that we only had to turn around to get to the other side and watch the outcome. But the current, if you could even call it that, was slow. Eventually, a stick emerged.

"You see?" said Rabbi Fred.

"Best two out of three?" I countered. He nodded, and we each gathered our additional entries. I tried to find sticks that were light but not too light, and long but not too long.

We met on the bridge again. Held sticks. Counted off. Dropped them in the water.

"Here's something I learned along the way," said Rabbi Fred as we waited and watched on the other side of the bridge. "Most people think that water currents and stick dimensions are what determine a stick's path. And, to a degree, that's true."

Splash!!

I turned, startled by the sound, and realized that Rabbi Fred must have picked up a big rock on the banks when we were selecting our sticks. The water sloshed, then rippled in all directions. Both of our sticks, which were emerging from under the bridge, reacted, but in different ways. One went left and ended up in a tangle of leaves trapped behind two boulders. The other went right, slid into the center of the current, and plowed ahead.

Guess whose stick got stuck?

"Interference!" I yelled.

Rabbi Fred held up his palms. "All right already. We can do a rematch. But you see what I mean, yes? One minute, you're going along on a path, and then all of a sudden, boom, there's a rock blocking your way or knocking you off course. And a rock like that can do a lot of damage."

I thought about it. What he was saying made sense. But what he was saying also made me want to throw rocks. So I got one off the banks, returned to the bridge, and threw.

Ke-splooosh!!

"You know how that makes me feel?" he asked.

"How?"

He grinned. "Like getting another rock."

So we both did, big ones.

"One, two, three!"

Ke-splash! Ke-sploosh!

I was headed to get another rock to throw when I noticed Rabbi Fred down at the edge of the water. I saw him gathering something, so instead of returning to the bridge, I went over to investigate.

"What are you doing?" I asked.

"This is the other part," he said. He had a bunch of small stones in one hand, and he used the other hand to carefully place them into the water, just downstream of where my stick had gotten stuck in the leaves. I realized he was creating sort of a makeshift wall. I took my big rock and placed it at one edge, and then we put several smaller stones next to it. One of the big boulders anchored our construction on the other side, so as we made the wall higher and higher, a funny thing happened. It was like a miniature version of one of the locks on the C&O Canal. The water in the little corner we'd formed rose higher and higher and slowly the leaves began to move and the next thing I knew my stick twirled back into the moving section of the current and headed downstream.

"Hey! We did it."

Rabbi Fred gave me a high five. Then he stuck his hands into the water, pulled out two flat stones, and gave one to me. "Think about this. You could say that the last stone was the one that sealed the deal, but in truth it wouldn't have succeeded without every single one beneath it and next to it. So just like one big rock can knock you off course, a lot of little rocks can boost you back on course."

"Is that how you got to be the stick-racing champion?"

"I'm actually talking about something, dare I say it, even bigger than stick racing. You know that song we sing sometimes at services? 'If I am not for myself, who will be for me? If I am only for myself, what am I? And if not now . . .' "

" 'If not now, when?' " I said, finishing his refrain.

"Exactly," said Rabbi Fred. "That song is based on the teachings of Hillel. Who was a brilliant rabbi. And, if I had to guess, probably a pretty formidable stick racer."

"So, you're saying I should try to be nicer to Noa?"

Rabbi Fred shrugged. "It wouldn't hurt. But it's more like a way of being in general. A way of seeing that the things you do and say can make a difference. For example, take your friend Dash. This might be a good time to ask yourself, *Am I doing all I can for him?*"

"I would, except I don't think he wants to hear from me right now," I admitted.

"You never know," he said. "Sometimes people who are grieving don't want to talk, but they usually appreciate knowing that people are thinking of them."

"Actually, I'm pretty sure he wants me to leave him alone. I tried texting him a bunch of times, but he didn't text me back. And then, the thing is . . ." I took a deep breath, studying the rock in my hand and trying to find the right words to explain what had happened. Why I read Dash's texts. Why I kept Dash's phone. Why I lied about it.

"Right, I know, he lost his phone," said Rabbi Fred, his voice startling me. I looked up at him. "I know this makes me a dinosaur, but I can't help pointing out that texting isn't the only way to reach out to a friend in need."

As he spoke, Rabbi Fred balanced his stone between his thumb and two fingers. He pulled back and skipped the rock across the creek. It bounced gracefully off the water's surface—one, two, three times—leaving ripples in its wake.

I positioned my own rock, then tried to copy his movements. One, two, three-four-*five* skips!

Rabbi Fred raised both eyebrows.

It felt good to see him impressed for the first time in a long time. Did I really want to come clean and watch his face fall? *Maybe I don't have to tell him anything,* I realized. *Maybe I just need to talk to Dash and make things right.*

"I think I get it," I said slowly. "You're saying I should just go up to Dash and, like, ask how he's doing."

Rabbi Fred stooped down, picked up a small reddish stone, and examined it. He polished it with the edge of his shirt, then slipped it into his pocket.

"That seems like a good place to start," he said.

Chapter Nine

At dinner that night, Karen told me she wanted to take me shopping at Mr. Maxx.

"We can go after school tomorrow," she suggested. "That way, we can find something for you to wear to Gil's unveiling this weekend. Plus, you'll probably need more clothes for all these bar and bat mitzvahs that are coming up."

"Gil's *unveiling*?" I asked nervously.

Enid clearly understood my tone. "His grave marker," she explained, helping herself to some salad.

"Right," said Karen. "It's a tradition—a little service at the cemetery to display the headstone after it's installed. Stacey sent an invitation, it's on the bulletin board. Didn't Dash mention it?"

"Sure," I lied. It felt easier than explaining that Dash was no longer talking to me.

"You know," added Jenny, reaching for the salad dressing, "if you want to ask Dash to come over afterward, that would be fine with us. You guys could even have a sleepover, if you want."

"We might even consider getting *soda,*" added Karen.

"Duht-DUH!" teased Enid.

Jenny leaned over and tried to grab Enid's nose with the salad tongs.

"Yeah, maybe," I said, pushing my food around my plate. My family was too busy joking to notice I wasn't eating or to hear how dejected I sounded. I appreciated the soda offer, but I didn't have the heart to tell my moms that not even the brilliant Dr Pepper had the skills to resuscitate my friendship with Dash.

When we went to Mr. Maxx, Karen bought me a whole bunch of clothes. Two pairs of pants that weren't jeans and didn't have a drawstring, plus one pair of "nice" sweatpants that she agreed could be worn in public as long as they were clean. I also got a pair of shoes that were not sneakers, two shirts with pointy collars, and exactly one tie. The tie was a compromise. I got to pick it out, as long as I was willing to wear it to services each and every Saturday. And to the unveiling.

I agreed, even though I had no intention of wearing my new tie to the unveiling. That was because I didn't plan on going to the unveiling. I knew Dash didn't want me there. And I figured the day would be hard enough without me showing up and making things worse for him. I was totally planning to talk to him, like I told Rabbi Fred. Just not yet and not there. Of course, I couldn't explain this to my moms, so I ended up pretending I didn't feel well. I was relieved when they bought it.

The following weekend was Eli Webb's bar mitzvah, so at nine-thirty in the morning, Enid actually got up early to do me a favor and tie my tie. She's explained the whole thing about the rabbit running around the tree to me several times, but it still comes out better when she does it. Facing me, yet not meeting my eye (due to her tie-tying responsibilities), Enid quizzed me on whether the phone had been returned to Dash.

"Not yet," I replied.

Enid frowned, examining the knot, then adjusting my collar.

"He's never at Hebrew school! So I haven't had the chance."

"Well, figure out another way. Seriously, Noah. It's time."

"I know, okay. Believe me, I want to," I told her, and not just because every time I saw any kind of pebble or rock, Rabbi Fred's words would come back to me. "Thanks," I added, because my tie looked good.

Yes, b'nei mitzvah season had begun—"with a vengeance," according to my moms. Their big gripe was the driving involved. Every weekend, one or two of my Hebrew school classmates were up, so I had to get to temple by ten (nine-forty-five if I had to "ush" and hand out programs). I had to sit through services, then go downstairs to the social hall, in the temple basement, for lunch. Usually, there'd be time to go home before the party, although sometimes the party would start right after services and go all afternoon. Either way, I had my moms' permission to remove the tie the minute they finished saying the hamotzi blessing over the challah bread.

I was excited for Eli's bar mitzvah. I had decided it would be the perfect place to strike up a casual conversation with Dash. If that went well, I could set down a well-placed rock or two—like asking him how he was feeling or offering to do something to help—and then maybe even tell him the funny story of how I inadvertently picked up his cell phone.

And there was another reason I was already looking forward to Eli's bar mitzvah. "Whoa," I'd said when the invitation arrived. "Check this out—instead of a regular party, they're taking everyone go-karting. Can we do that for mine?"

"We'll talk," said Karen, pinning the invitation to the bulletin board in our kitchen with the others and making a note on the family calendar. No wonder I never saw the invitation Stacey sent for the unveiling—

our bulletin board had been taken over by big, shiny square and rectangular, and, in Eli's case, car-shaped invitations.

The go-karting was to take place right after services ended, so after the hamotzi, all the girls ran to change clothes while we guys pulled off our ties and played something between Frisbee and football in the front hall with the leftover red satin yarmulkes with Eli's name on them. Eli's parents had rented a bus, so when it arrived, we all piled on board.

"Take any available seat!" Eli's dad yelled from the front of the bus. "Please, we need to get going."

Behind me, someone pushed, so I ended up in the very back by the bathroom. Sitting with Chris Stern, of all people. He was probably bummed not to be sitting with Dash, too.

At the go-kart track place, a ridiculously cheerful woman called Safety Sam made us watch a safety video. And then we had to listen to all the same rules again from a similarly perky guy named Safety Steve. It was a lot like school, with the girls raising their hands because they knew the answers from paying attention. Next we had to put on these things they called head socks and helmets. I really wanted to riff with Dash on the idea of head socks ("What's next, foot hats? Am I right?"), but he was standing as far away from me as humanly possible.

There were too many of us to race all at once, so they grouped us into heats. I was glad that by some miracle

Dash and I got put in the same heat, even though Noa was in it, too. She was fussing because she has so much hair that it was hard for her to put on the head sock. When she finally got it on, she had to use both hands to hold it in place while Dash helped her put her helmet on over it.

The actual go-kart track was the coolest thing ever! They had signs up all over that literally read NO SPEED LIMIT! But during the safety briefing, Safety Steve kept saying again and again that bumping or trying to crash was strictly prohibited. They had all these different-colored flags, not just the usual checkerboard one. Yellow, blue, green, and black—each meant something. I wasn't actually paying attention at that part, except I did hear him say that black meant you were being placed in a time-out for breaking the rules. We weren't in the first heat, so we got to see the black flag in action a bunch of times before we were up. The yellow flag seemed to be a warning that came right before black.

Finally, it was time for our heat. I looked around for Dash and saw him climbing into car #40 as Noa got into #36 right behind him. I grabbed #17, strapped myself in, and awaited the horn I had heard at the start of each of the previous heats.

HWAAAAAAAAARRRRRNNNN!

I tore off the instant the horn blasted and quickly overtook two of the seven cars in our heat, neither of which was Dash's. I leaned into the turn, enjoying the speed and the noise of the engine racing. I could see #40 up ahead, and I tried to predict where he'd be in the next turn so I could pull alongside him. It had already occurred to me that it would be tough to have a real conversation at however many miles per hour we were going. Plus, it was really hard to hear because of the loud go-kart engines, the head socks and helmets covering our ears, and the cheering spectators (okay, most of the kids who weren't racing were ignoring the action on the track, but Eli's grandma seemed really into it). I didn't have a plan for how to deal with this. I just figured I'd pull up and drive next to him for a lap or two and wing it. Maybe I could yell out that line from the mustard commercial—that'd crack him up. And even if it was too loud to hear me, at least he'd see me next to him and that might remind him of how much fun we used to have together.

That's the thing about being best friends: you don't always have to talk. But if you do want to talk about stuff, you can. Especially late at night on sleepovers, just before you fall asleep. I remembered the time I told Dash how me and Enid weren't technically related, like by blood. And he told me that sometimes he wished he didn't have a brother, because before Pete came along, his parents didn't used to fight so much. Then he said he wished I were his brother instead of Pete, and I said, "Me too." We fell asleep making a plan for a time machine that would take us back to before Pete was born.

That sleepover felt like a long time ago. It felt like time was going so fast—maybe because I was going so fast, whizzing around the speedway faster than I intended and actually passing Dash's car at the corner, which was not what I wanted. I tried to slow my car a little so we'd be side by side, but there was another car behind me. And a flag flying in my face, a blue one being waved by Safety Sam, who was leaning over the railing in a way that didn't look safe at all. I wondered if she and Safety Steve were related, or if Steve and Sam were even their real names. It would've been particularly funny if they were twins and their mom was such a safety nut that she actually named them Safety Steve and Safety Sam and gave them little fluorescent yellow safety vests to wear with their diapers. That could've made a hilarious comedy sketch. . . . I wished I could tell Dash about it. Maybe after I—

TWEEETTTTTT!!!

A whistle sounded really loudly. I guessed it was because someone was breaking one of the rules, but I couldn't stop to see who because Dash's car was sliding into position next to me. I hit the accelerator to keep pace with him, and turned to grin at him, but the next thing I knew, there was a car in front of me that came out of nowhere and I had to scramble for the brake.

Except the brake wasn't where I thought it would be, so when I pressed a pedal, my car shot forward *FAST.*

Right into the car in front of me.

Car #36. Noa's car.

Errrrrrrrrr!!!

Augggghhhhh!!!

CRUNCHHHHH!!!!

That was the horrible noise my car made as it skidded toward car #36, and the terrified scream I let out as my car collided with car #36, and the sickening sound I heard as my car tumbled over car #36. Somewhere in there, I let go of the steering wheel and covered my face, which might have prevented me from breaking my nose when my face hit the steering wheel as my car flipped. I opened my eyes to find myself still strapped in, on my side, facing the Plexiglass guardrail. Looking down at me was Eli's grandma, who no longer seemed as gung ho about go-karting.

I immediately thought of *Cool Runnings,* the John Candy movie about the Jamaican bobsled team, and how every time they crashed, one of the guys would ask his friend, "Ya dead?" I was pretty sure I couldn't be dead because I could feel my heart pounding. I hoped no one else was dead, either. That would be more than I could take.

Someone—not one of the Safety siblings—ran over to unbuckle me and make sure I was okay. Meanwhile, everyone else—both Safeties, Eli's parents, and the kids in our Hebrew school class, including Dash (who had pulled over when our heat came to a crashing halt)—ran to check on Noa. She stood up unsteadily, then removed her helmet, then her head sock. Her frizzy red hair exploded out of it, and she gave it a tentative shake. Leaning on Dash, she hobbled off the track while everyone cheered.

No one clapped for me. And when Safety Steve was done making sure Noa was okay, he came over to tell me that I had to sit in the time-out zone until they served refreshments.

"But I didn't break any rules. It was an accident."

"You crashed, dude," said Safety Steve, a.k.a. Captain Obvious. "That's a rule violation in and of itself."

I felt a flash of anger. *Don't call me dude.* "I thought yellow was the warning one," I protested.

"It is, but the blue flag is the one that means it isn't safe to pass. We covered that in the safety training. And the video," he added pointedly.

Great, I thought miserably when the next heat started up and I was alone on the time-out bench. No yellow warning flag, no nothing. Just rolling along and then, when you least expect it, *wham!* Just like life.

Or, more accurately, just like death.

I know I should have been happy to be alive and well and sitting on a bench. I mean, consider the alternative. I could have been pining for the fjords. But surviving the crash meant a front-row seat to watch Noa and Eli and Chris and everyone having a blast without me. Even Dash, who was laughing and smiling, too. It didn't seem like he was missing his dad at all. It seemed like he had forgotten all about him.

* * *

When the go-kart party was finally over, I saw Frau Blue Car pull into the parking lot. I ran to get in.

"Hey," I said, surprised.

"What?" said Enid.

"I just—you never pick me up."

"Okay, well, remind me never to do it again."

"No, I didn't mean—"

Enid laughed. "I'm just messing with you."

I slid down in my seat and watched as Noa and Dash both got into Dash's mom's car.

"Hey, what happened?"

"Huh?" I put my hand up because she was staring at my forehead. When I touched the Band-Aid, I realized that maybe I looked worse than I felt. I looked in the mirror on the passenger side. *Yikes!* In addition to the bandage, I was sporting a black eye. No wonder Safety Steve had offered me a frozen hamburger patty. He laughed when I asked him if I could have it medium-rare instead, but I wasn't kidding.

"Oh, it's nothing," I said, trying to play it cool, even as I became increasingly aware that my head actually kind of hurt. "I got into a crash with another go-kart, but I'm okay."

"Wow, sounds like quite the bar mitzvah," said Enid.

"I guess," I said glumly.

"Once more with feeling," Enid teased. "Any swag?"

I pulled out a red drawstring backpack emblazoned with GO, ELI, GO! plus a Star of David with go-kart wheels and the date on it. I yanked a matching red T-shirt out of it and held it up for her to see.

Enid whistled appreciatively. "In my day," she said, "you might get a bag or a shirt, but *both*?"

"What did you give out?" I asked her.

"Paperwhites."

"Paperweights?" I could totally see that: our moms handing out painted rocks or lumpy chunks of clay as party favors.

"Not paperweights, you dork. Paper*whites*," said Enid. "They're bulbs. You put them in gravel with a little bit of water in the winter, and they set down roots and these pretty green stalks and white flowers come up. They're cool and they smell nice."

"Our moms sent people home with plants after your bat mitzvah?" I asked.

"I didn't have a bat mitzvah, remember?" Enid corrected me. "But I had a thirteenth birthday party, which the moms decided should be called a 'not mitzvah' as a joke. You don't remember this?"

I shook my head. "I was, what, six?"

"More like eight, but same diff. It was a million years ago," said Enid. "We gave everyone a paperwhite bulb in a little cup of gravel wrapped with tissue paper and with some sort of a poem Karen found about patience and blooming and stuff." She laughed. "Ivan

Metz-Peterson told everyone the poem was about boobs, not flowers."

"Seriously?" I asked. Ivan was my friend Adam from Hebrew school's big brother.

"Yup," she said. "How is Adam?"

"He's okay," I said. I was about to tell her how he drank three Slurpees in a row, announced he had a brain freeze, then threw up purple, when she casually asked, "Was Dash there?"

"Yeah," I said.

"Did you get a chance to give him his phone?"

"No," I admitted. "I was going to, but I couldn't just, like, hand it to him. I needed to talk to him first, and there just wasn't a good time."

To my relief, Enid nodded. "Makes sense. He's gotta be a total train wreck right now."

"Train wreck" made me think of my go-kart crash and how, once again, I'd ended up making everything worse for everyone around me. And this time I hadn't even opened my mouth!

Enid continued. "I mean, the unveiling was just last weekend. That had to be hard for him. It takes a lot longer than you might think to get over something like this."

"Tell me about it," I said.

Enid poked at the radio, trying to find a good station. I could tell she was waiting for me to elaborate. Sometimes it bugs me that she always knows when I have more to say, but right then it didn't.

"This might sound weird," I told her, "but you know how you sort of have a dad?"

"I don't 'sort of' have a dad," said Enid. "Howard's a real dad, he's just not a particularly spectacular one."

"Right, but here's the thing. I don't even have a crappy one," I said. "And Gil was a really good dad and, like, a total mensch. And he treated me just like he did Dash. So now that he's gone, I miss him, too, okay?"

"I get it," said Enid.

"Can you do me a favor and not tell the moms about this?" I asked. "I mean, just because I miss Gil doesn't mean I don't love them or appreciate—"

"Noah, stop. You're going to make me throw up."

"Okay," I said warily.

"This is just between you and me. Really." She took her eyes off the road for a split second to lock gazes with me before turning back.

We drove on without talking for a while.

"You missed our turn," I pointed out.

Enid didn't answer. Instead, she reached over to turn up the music and said, "Shhh, I love this song. Check it out, this is Disturbed." I must have heard her wrong, because it definitely didn't sound like her favorite band. But the slow, eerie tune was familiar to me. I couldn't quite make out the words until Enid started singing along.

Hello, darkness, my old friend.
I've come to talk with you again. . . .

I definitely knew the song, but I had never heard this version before. And I guess I had never paid much attention to the lyrics.

And the vision that was planted in my brain
Still remains
Within the sound of silence.

I didn't realize it was such a weird and creepy song, almost to the point of being scary. And the words made no sense whatsoever. How can darkness be a friend? Silence doesn't have any sound—isn't that the whole point? I closed my eyes, listening to the haunting melody and waiting for the song to end so I could raise these questions with Enid.

But I must have dozed off, because the next thing I knew, the car had slowed down and made a sharp turn. I opened my eyes as Enid pulled into a parking lot and turned off the engine.

"Where are we?" I asked. We were next to a big park, with an iron gate, tall old trees, winding stone paths, and lots and lots of gravestones. "Wait, is this—?"

Enid got out of the car, then leaned back in the open door and asked, "You coming?"

"Sure," I said, though the real answer was, *I don't know.* I was scared to get out of the car, but even more scared to sit in it all alone at the cemetery.

Together we walked through the iron gate. It didn't occur to me until we were pretty far down one of the paths that I wasn't observing the not-polite-to-breathe rule. On reflex, I sucked in my breath. But then I let it out again, in one big whoosh. It was a cold day, so the puff of breath hung in the air for a split second, almost like a ghost.

Without thinking, I did it again. Enid did, too. She must have had the same idea, because she went "Woooo," so I did, too. And for a moment we just stood there, making ghosts back and forth at each other. But then I started laughing at the idea of making ghosts with your breaths, and it felt a lot less scary. Like if it weren't for all the grave markers, Enid and I could be taking a walk in a regular park. There were lots of trees and, probably because it was cold out, barely any people. I zipped my jacket all the way up and shoved my hands in my pockets, and Enid took off the long beaded scarf she was wearing and wrapped it around me, and we kept on walking.

And then we walked down a little path and there it was. At first I was surprised that Enid knew how to find it. It's not like there were maps and signs, like at the zoo. And the burial had been for immediate family only. But it dawned on me that she must have gone to the unveiling. Because she had walked us straight to it: Gil's grave.

There was a big gray stone marking it. The sides were rough but the front was polished and said GILBERT LOUIS BLUM. It had the date he was born and the date he died and a Star of David. And one line under it.

" 'Always with us,' " I read. It was true. Gil was always on my mind, it seemed, whether I liked it or not.

"Yeah," said Enid. "At the unveiling, Stacey said that what Gil actually wanted it to say was, 'There goes the neighborhood.' Apparently, that's what Rodney Dangerfield's headstone says. But she couldn't bring herself to do it."

I couldn't help smiling at Gil's last joke. Even though the thought of planning out what you wanted your gravestone to say seemed like the saddest thing ever.

"I'm going to walk around a little," said Enid.

"I'll come with you," I offered.

"Hang out here for a few," instructed Enid. I must have looked worried, because she added, "I won't go far, I promise."

"What am I supposed to do?" I asked.

"That's up to you." She added, "At a minimum, just breathe. I promise no one will mind."

She winked, then walked off, and I stood there awkwardly. I considered sitting down, but that felt weird. Maybe it was perfectly fine to breathe when other people couldn't, but that didn't necessarily mean it was polite to sit on them. So I examined the headstone and took a closer look at the small rocks sitting on top of it. If each little stone represented one person coming by, there'd been at least ten visitors. Maybe twenty. I guessed I should probably leave one, too. Only I didn't see any stones on the ground. And it definitely seemed wrong to take one off another gravestone and move it to Gil's.

It occurred to me that it didn't make sense that you always leave the same thing when you visit a Jewish person's grave: rocks. Why not something that said something about that particular person? Like something they'd actually miss.

"So, how are you doing?" I whispered. I paused, terrified of getting a response. But since Gil's gravestone, obviously, didn't jump in, I started talking again to fill the silence. It felt a little weird to be having a conversation with a big slab of granite, but it felt weirder not to. "I'm doing okay," I said. "Sorry I didn't bring you a rock, but I didn't actually expect to be here today." Again, no answer.

It felt a little frustrating to talk and not get anything back. It reminded me of Gil's stupid Magic 8 Ball. REPLY HAZY, TRY AGAIN. REPLY HAZY, TRY AGAIN. REPLY HAZY, TRY AGAIN.

Why should I try again?

And what had I done to deserve the sound of silence? From Dash. But even more so from Gil. Gil had done the unthinkable. The unforgivable. He had imposed the permanent silent treatment.

I was freezing, standing there, even with Enid's scarf. But I also felt a cold, dark anger rising inside of me. I kicked my feet a little to warm up, and I was surprised at how dangerous and wrong—

and irresistible—

it felt to kick Gil's gravestone. Just a little.

Kick. *For going and leaving.*

Kick. Kick. *For not saying goodbye.*

Kick—a harder one that time—*for making Dash hate me.*

Kick! *For making me think you cared when you obviously didn't. About me or Dash or anyone but yourself.*

Kick!! Kick!! *For being selfish! Really REALLY selfish!*

"Noah?"

I froze, foot on stone.

"You okay?"

I looked up, embarrassed. Enid was standing there, watching me from several graves away.

"I'm pretty cold," she said. "So, you know. Whenever?"

I nodded. I touched my toe to Gil's gravestone one more time. This time less of a kick and more of a foot bump. Sort of like Gil and Dash's sidekick bit.

Tap. *I'm still mad. But I'm also still your dude.*

I gestured to Enid. I was ready to go.

"You okay?" she said as we walked back to the car.

"Yeah," I said. Then I remembered something. "Hey, you don't by any chance happen to have, like, a rock?"

Enid dug around in her pockets for a minute. Then

she pulled out something wrapped in a napkin, peeked at it, and held it out to me.

"Just this," she said. "It's kind of rocklike."

"Perfect," I said. I ran back and set it on Gil's headstone, then returned to join my sister for the drive home.

I wondered who would be the first to discover, sitting there among all the similar small gray stones, a larger, misshapen item that on closer inspection turned out not to be a rock at all. It might be a bird, giving it a curious peck. Or a squirrel. Or a person. But it felt good to know that in that whole cemetery, there was only one gravestone marked with a collection of rocks . . . and one rock-hard, extremely salty vegan cookie.

Gil definitely would have liked that.

Next time, I decided, I would bring him a can of seltzer.

On the drive home, Enid cranked up her music, which was a relief because it meant I didn't have to explain why I'd tried to beat up a gravestone. When we finally got home, she gave me a quick hug, but she kept her distance after we got out of the car. I appreciated that because I could tell it was so our moms wouldn't suspect anything was up and pester her for details.

We walked into the house silently, first her, then me. Our moms, who were both sitting on the couch, looked up. I had almost completely forgotten about the go-kart party until I saw their eyes widen at the sight of my face.

"Jeez Louise, Noah, what happened to you?" asked Karen.

Chapter Ten

Dash didn't come back to Hebrew school for several weeks. Every week I would bring his phone, fully charged (thank you, brown rice!), and every week it would stay in my backpack and go home with me again. It was sort of demoralizing to not even have the opportunity to try to give it back to him, but it was also sort of a relief. In theory, I could have brought it to one of the bar or bat mitzvahs on the weekends. But I heard from Adam and Jared and Eli that Dash hadn't been showing up at them, either, so I had a lot less incentive to go myself. Without Dash, especially after the go-kart disaster, even the promise of a chocolate fountain was not enough to tempt me.

In terms of my own bar mitzvah, there was no way to hide from Noa because she was my partner. To be fair, after I apologized for crashing into her go-kart (and threw in a bonus apology for that day on snack duty), she wasn't going out of her way to talk to me, but she wasn't being a total jerk, either. We didn't work on our Three Stooges project much because Dash wasn't at Hebrew school and Noa was still of the view that it wasn't kosher to leave him out. So instead, we took turns reading our parsha out loud and trying to transition from doing the much easier Hebrew text with the vowels to the vowel-less version, like we'd have to when we read from the actual Torah scrolls on the big day.

"That was good," she admitted after I stumbled through an entire three-sentence chunk without vowels.

"Yeah, well, maybe I won't totally embarrass you on our big day," I said. I kind of set her up for putting me down. I mean, she could have easily slammed me with a comment like "You mean you won't be there?" or something like that.

Instead, she just pointed down to the study sheet.

"Try the next one," she suggested.

"But that one's yours," I said, double-checking the spreadsheet to make sure.

Noa shrugged. "It doesn't have to be," she said. If she were anyone else, I would have accused her of trying to dump work on me. But this was clearly her version of a compliment.

* * *

Two nights later, Jenny and Karen took me to see something called Voices of Now at Arena Stage, a theater on the other side of D.C. They said it was something Stacey had suggested we check out. I was game both because I like live performances and because I'd successfully argued for the right to wear my new sweatpants (on the theory that I'd need to keep my temple pants clean for the upcoming weekend's service-and-party combo). We got there and found seats in the back. The theater's walls, floor, seats, and stage were black. The only color was on a banner at the back of the stage with the words VOICES OF NOW on it in big blue letters. I still didn't know what the name meant. I hoped, but kind of doubted, that Voices of Now might be a comedy showcase.

"Hey, is that Stacey?" I asked Jenny, pointing to a woman sitting several rows ahead of us. It was hard to see because the theater was dark and getting darker, since the performance was about to start, but Jenny squinted and agreed that it looked like her. And not only that, it looked as if Dash and Pete were sitting there with her. I hadn't seen Pete or Stacey since the shiva, a couple of months earlier. Pete still looked really little, but he wasn't jumping around like he always used to. Maybe he had a toy or something to keep him quiet—I couldn't tell from where we were sitting.

The curtain went up and two people came onstage. They introduced themselves as Amanda and Fahrid. "We're the directors of the play you're about to see," Amanda explained. "It was created through a partnership with the Wendt Center for Loss and Healing. With this particular ensemble, we are able to work with young people who have experienced a loss and are grieving."

Uh-oh. This was definitely not going to be a comedy showcase.

"In the process of developing this play," Fahrid added, "we discovered that grief brings up a lot of questions. And it led us to an investigation of what we do with those questions that others have for us. And how grief changes over time."

Everyone clapped, including us, and as they left the stage, the lights faded to black again. When the lights and some music came up, six kids that looked to be my age or a few years older were standing on the stage. Four of the kids were black and two were white. Three were boys, three were girls. And then I looked more closely at the girls.

And I realized that the one in the middle was Noa.

She didn't speak at first. Instead, a boy with glasses crouched in the center of the stage while the other five kids faced him. The music faded and one of the other kids, a girl with lots of long braids, spoke to him.

"How are you?" she asked.

"Are you okay?" asked another boy, much taller than the one crouching in the middle. He looked like a basketball player.

"Are you sure you're okay?" asked Noa.

"This isn't happening, I wish this weren't happening," said the kid in the middle, not answering any of the questions.

A girl with a blond ponytail then pretended to pack a bag. She walked by each of the other kids as they said things to her like "Everything's going to be okay" and "Do you want to be alone?" and "You should celebrate his life!" She groaned at the last statement and ran to the other side of the stage.

As the play went on, the kids came forward one by one and spoke directly to the audience, telling about their experiences losing someone they loved. All of their stories were really sad. One boy's dad was killed by somebody trying to rob his store. The blond girl's older brother overdosed. The boy who looked like a basketball player said his mom came to all his games, even in a wheelchair, until she got so sick she couldn't anymore. Then, one morning, she didn't wake up and he had to call 911. After a while, almost all the kids had talked, so it seemed like the play might be nearly over.

And then Noa stepped forward.

Noa talked about how she barely knew her dad because he died when she was so small. She talked about how she wasn't sure whether she could trust her memories or if she was just making things up in her head to make herself feel better. Then she began to talk about her grandpa. I hadn't known that he'd died, too, just eight months earlier. He had been like a dad to her, especially before her mom remarried. They were really close and she used to talk to him almost every day. Now he was gone, and not only did she miss him, she said, but losing him made her miss her dad even more.

The other kids leaned in to ask questions and offer suggestions, like they'd done before. Initially, I thought the questions were pretty thoughtful and sincere. I could see that the kids telling their stories found them intrusive, but at first it seemed like maybe they were being overly sensitive.

But after I'd listened to Noa talk about her grandpa, the whole thing kind of shifted for me. Jenny's dad died before I was born, and Karen's dad, Grandpa Joe, was still alive, but he had dementia, so now he lived in a nursing home on Long Island, not far from where he had lived with Grandma Beth. I remembered fishing with him, and asking Grandma Beth why he couldn't come fishing with us anymore. I missed fishing with Grandpa Joe, and I missed having banana sword fights with Gil, and I started thinking about all the things I would never get to do again. And then I thought about Dash and Pete and all the things they'd never get to do at all. Like having their dad called up to the bimah for an aliyah at their bar mitzvahs, which is one of those honors grown-ups seem to love. Not that Gil was super-religious. He was always goofing around with us at temple. He'd sing the song "Ma Tovu" as "My Tofu" just to crack us up. But somehow I always imagined that at Dash's bar mitzvah he'd be the proudest guy in the room.

Except he wasn't going to be in that room—or any room—ever again.

So now, when the kids onstage said, "Are you okay?" I felt like they were talking to me. When they said, "Do you need anything?" the hair was standing up on my arms, and when they said, "Why don't you look sad?" I wanted to jump up on the stage myself and yell at them. And cry. And apologize to Dash and Noa and Enid and my moms and everyone for everything wrong I'd ever done.

When the play ended, we gave the cast a standing ovation.

"That was phenomenal," said Jenny. Karen and I nodded in agreement, still clapping hard. It wasn't like any other play I had ever seen. It was sad, but it wasn't depressing. And there was humor in it, too, even though I wouldn't tell someone it was a funny play. Most of all, it was clear that all the kids in the play had done something really brave by getting up there and telling us what it was like for them. I felt grateful to all of them for it, even though I only knew one of them.

After the play, there was a reception in the lobby with fruit punch and cookies. I said hi to Noa and her parents, then looked for my moms again. I found them talking to Stacey, who gave me a big hug.

"Noah, it's so good to see you! And you're getting so tall," she told me.

"Really?" I asked, pulling myself up to my full height.

"Uh-huh," said Stacey, but instead of looking at me, she was glancing around the room. "I'm sorry—Dash is in the car already. He's missed some school, so he has a lot of homework to catch up on. I just need to find Pete so we can get going."

"Oh, yeah, no problem," I said. "Say hey to Dash for me. Is he, uh, doing okay?"

Stacey gave me this really grateful smile. "He's doing much better, Noah. Thanks so much for asking."

"Sure," I said. One stone, successfully placed.

"Actually, Noah, can you do me a favor?" asked Stacey. "Can you look in the boys' room for Pete?"

"Of course," I told her, pleased to be asked. Rabbi Fred was right. There were lots of opportunities for small, well-placed stones. I went to the restroom and looked under all the stall doors. No feet. I was about to leave when I thought I heard something. I went back and checked again. One stall was locked, and if I squinted through the crack along the door, I could see that there was someone in there, hiding.

"Pete?" I called.

No response.

"Pete, hey, it's Noah. Your mom says it's time to go."

"Not going."

Okay, at least I got a response. Now we were getting somewhere. I remembered how me and Dash used to try to convince Gil we were starting SND without him to get him to come downstairs faster. "Pete, they're serving ice cream out here," I tried. "Quadruple-scoop cones, you're gonna miss it, man. I'm gonna have to eat yours. It's pistachio, cookie dough, tutti-frutti, and fudge ripple with gummy bears on top."

"Not. Coming. Out."

"Fine, okay," I said. And then I had another idea. "In fact, I'm going to stay here, too. It's very comfy. I'll just sleep with my head here in the urinal. Oh, look! They left a big, delicious mint on my pillow."

A giggle escaped from under the stall door.

"Hey . . . munch, munch, crunch . . . wait a second . . . this isn't a mint . . . this is . . . gahhhhh!!!!" I screamed, and ran for the sink, pretending to frantically wash my mouth out. "Gahhhhh!" I continued to wail, making gargling noises until I heard the door unlatch and Pete's little face appear.

"You didn't really eat it," he accused.

"I did too, and you know what I'm going to eat next? You!" I did my best monster claws and lunged at him, and he shrieked with laughter. I picked him up and hauled him over one shoulder, at which point he announced, "Piggyback!"

"Works for me," I said.

Triumphantly, we galloped out of the bathroom.

Stacey looked very relieved when we appeared. "Peter Blum, where were you? You need to let me know if you want to go somewhere."

The only problem? Pete refused to dismount.

"Is it okay if I take him to their car?" I asked Jenny.

"By all means," said Jenny. "We'll go get Frau Blue Car and meet you in front of the theater."

"Wow," said Stacey. "Petey, today is your lucky day."

On the way to their parking spot, Stacey leaned in and whispered, "Thank you so much, Noah. Pete really needed this."

"No problem," I told her.

As we walked up, I could see Dash sitting in the passenger seat. It occurred to me that maybe he'd think his mom made me come to the car to say hi. My moms do things like that sometimes and it drives me nuts. So when he got out of the car, the first thing I said was, "Don't worry, your mom didn't make me come here."

"Noah ate the pee-pee cake!" Pete announced, jumping off my back.

"Get in the car, Pete," Dash said in kind of a snarly voice. And then, while his mom helped Pete get buckled in, Dash came around the back of the car to where I was. "We don't need your help," he said.

I stared at him. "Your mom asked me to help," I said.

"Sure," said Dash.

"She did! What's your problem?" I asked.

"I don't have a problem," said Dash. His arms were folded tightly across his chest, with his fingers jammed in his armpits. Which reminded me of the time he was on crutches.

"Well, I do!" I said. "I miss him, too."

"That's just it," said Dash, pulling his hands out and balling them into fists. "This is not about you. He wasn't your dad, okay? And Pete's not your brother."

"I know that."

Stacey emerged from the back seat and slammed the door, maybe to get our attention. "Boys?" she said. "Everything okay?"

"Yeah," grumbled Dash. Stacey got in the driver's seat and started the engine.

"Look, I know we can't pretend nothing's changed," I told Dash. "But would it *kill* you to just talk to me? Sorry!" Instinctively, I cringed because, once again, I had tossed the k-word out without thinking.

"That's just it!" he said, throwing up his hands.

"What? I said I was sorry."

"Stop walking on eggshells around me. Kill! Die! Death! See? I can take it."

"So, you're okay talking about your dad's death?"

"Sometimes. When I want. With who I want."

"Okay, fine. I get it," I said. "I guess I should be glad you have Chris to talk to."

Dash tilted his head to one side. "Who's Chris?" he asked.

"Chris Stern. Your new best friend?"

"I don't know what you're talking about."

"Dash. I know!"

"Know what?"

Stacey leaned her head out the window. "Dash, hon?" she called. "It's late, and I need to get Pete to bed. Can you guys maybe continue your conversation another time?"

"Sure! Sorry," I said, watching Dash get in the car. I really wanted to prove to him that I knew about Chris.

And then all of a sudden I realized I could. I walked up to the passenger side and knocked. Before he could roll the window down, I pulled Dash's phone out of my pocket and held it up. I figured he'd roll down his window and I could explain.

"I'm sorry," I'd say. "I found it and I meant to give it back right away, honest, but I didn't. I made some bad choices, but I want you to know that everything I did, I did for a good reason. I just should have told you sooner. And I hope that, eventually, you'll forgive me." Maybe he'd be mad—who could blame him? But he'd have to give me some credit for trying to do the honorable thing and make things right. I'd keep carefully placing small stones and rebuilding our friendship. And before long, Rabbi Fred would see us in the hallways at Hebrew school goofing around like old times. I could already see him giving me a knowing wink for showing myself to be such a good, responsible person. Such a mensch.

But none of that happened. Instead, through the closed window, I saw Dash see his phone in my hand just as Stacey pulled away from the curb.

"Wait! I just need to—" I called, but it was too late for Dash or his mom to hear me. So I ended up standing there with the phone in my hand, realizing that I had neither carefully placed nor gracefully skipped this particular stone. Instead, my rock had landed with a deafening splash, sloshing water in every direction and knocking everything off course, including me.

Especially me.

Chapter Eleven

When we got home Thursday night, I saw that the light was still on in Enid's room. So I went and caught her up on everything. Meaning: seeing Noa in the play, helping Stacey with Pete, finally getting to talk to Dash, showing him the phone . . . and not quite successfully returning it to him.

Enid put her face in her hands and groaned.

"I don't believe this," she said.

"I know, E! I was trying to give it back. But then Stacey drove off and I missed my chance."

"Noah, how long have you had that phone?"

"I know, all right," I said. "I just wanted to talk to him first. But when I tried to, he acted all mad and pretended he never even *talked* to Chris, much less told him about his dad."

"So?!" Enid's eyes flashed with anger. "Maybe he didn't want anyone to know—not even you. Isn't he allowed to decide who he confides in?"

"I mean, I guess, but—"

Enid ran her hands up the shaved sides of her head, shaking the long purple hair on top into her eyes. "Noah, think about it. This stuff is really hard to talk about. There was a piece just the other day on NPR—" She caught herself and covered her mouth. "Oh no, I'm turning into my mom!"

"It's okay, go on," I said.

"It was about survivors' guilt, which people who are close to someone who kills himself often experience. They feel guilty for not seeing warning signs. And they obsess over things the person said or did in the days leading up to the suicide, trying to figure out what they could have done differently."

"Oh," I said, thinking about wishing for a do-over. And dreaming about trying to pull Gil out of a raging river.

"Yeah, so, put yourself in Dash's shoes. And while you're at it, think about how much pressure he probably feels to try to set a good example for Pete. He probably thinks that now he has to act like a dad instead of just a brother. Even though, last I checked, he's only twelve."

"And a half," I added.

Enid snorted ruefully. "You need to try again, Noah, to apologize—and I don't mean for just taking his phone."

"I didn't *take* it," I started to say, but she waved her hands at me, making it clear that she didn't want to hear it.

"It's the right thing to do. Besides," she added, "if he tells the rabbis, you're toast."

I went to Hebrew school the following Tuesday determined to return Dash's phone and fix everything, no matter what. It was the right thing to do. I was ready to do it. And it was time to do it.

Ideally, before the rabbis found out.

My plan was to confront Dash, offer him the apology of the century, and beg for his forgiveness. For old times' sake, I decided to bring a banana and offer to fall on my banana sword. That was perfect. It was totally going to work.

It had to work. And I was in luck—for once, Dash was actually there.

I set my plan into action the minute Dash walked in at the beginning of skills class. First, I was on my best behavior so Rabbi Jake wouldn't need to speak with me after class. Then, as soon as the break started, I ran downstairs and put my name and Dash's on the sign-up sheet for electives. This was something we always used to do—signing up each other without talking about it first, because it didn't matter what elective we did as long as we could be in it together.

And finally, when I went to get a snack, I grabbed my banana out of my backpack and timed it perfectly so I was right in front of Dash in the snack line. The sixth graders were in charge of selling today.

"Rice cakes or popcorn?" A girl selling snacks held up both options.

"Um, popcorn," I told her.

"What's with the banana?" she asked.

"I don't know," I said loudly, for Dash's benefit. "I wasn't expecting the Spanish Inquisition."

The girl looked at me, puzzled.

I turned and noticed that Dash was no longer behind me. He must have left the line without getting a snack. I paid for my snack, then waited for Dash to come back to the social hall, hopefully before electives started. When he didn't return, I finished my popcorn and then, forgetting my plan, ate my banana. I tossed the peel in the direction of the can but missed. I've never been great at basketball (or any game involving a ball, for that matter). Clearly, apologizing wasn't turning out to be my sport, either.

Unfortunately, I had been in such a hurry to make sure we got the same elective that I didn't notice what I'd signed us up for. You guessed it: Israeli dance. Still, I convinced myself that this might be okay. The good thing about Israeli dance is that, unlike a discussion elective, you don't have to sit in your seat and pay attention. You can move around and have side conversations while the music is playing—provided you're not learning a new dance, which is almost never the case. When the bell rang for electives to start, I saw Dash come out of the bathroom, head for the stairs, and get stopped by Rabbi Fred, who showed him the sign-up sheet. Dash looked irritated, but he turned around and returned to the social hall, where I was, along with Noa, Chris Stern, Deena, Sarah, Maya, and about ten other kids, mostly girls. For some reason, a lot of the girls can't get enough of Israeli dance.

The first song started up.

"Forecast: no rain in sight. Time for everybody's favorite . . . Mayim Mayim!" called Solly. Since we almost always did this dance, we all knew we were supposed to hold hands and dance in a circle. I found a spot next to Dash, and we did what we guys always do, which is pull our sleeves over our palms so we don't actually have to have our hands touch. As we began to move, I leaned in and caught Dash's eye.

"Hey, can I talk to you?" I asked. Dash looked at me as if I'd just arrived on a spaceship from another galaxy. And said nothing.

Great. More silent treatment. A couple of the girls were looking at us with concern. Possibly because Solly was yelling "Reverse! Go the other way!" but neither Dash nor I had changed direction, so we were having some minor collisions with other people in the circle.

"Grapevine!" yelled Solly.

Crud. I was terrible at grapevine and often messed up, even while staring at my feet. Still, I didn't really have a choice. Meanwhile, I tried again with Dash.

"Just hear me out," I said.

"What?" said Dash impatiently.

"Ow!" said the girl on the other side of me, whose foot I had apparently stepped on.

"Sorry," I told her, which made me remember that the person I was supposed to be apologizing to was Dash. So I turned to him and added, "I just wanted to say I'm sorry about the way I acted the other night, after the play." Step, "Sorry!" step, step. "And about keeping your phone and everything." I probably should have stopped, but instead I added, "You don't have to accept my apology right now, but I'm kind of hoping that eventually you'll stop hating me."

Dash didn't say anything, so I kept on going.

"You know what? I don't even care," I told him. Step, step, "Sorry!" step. "If it makes you feel better to hate me, go ahead."

"Boys, zip it!" yelled Solly. "*Mayim, mayim, mayim, mayim,* CLAP!" he yelled as we all rushed forward toward the center of the circle.

Dash kept his eyes down. Possibly because he was trying to make his feet work—he's almost as bad a dancer as I am. Finally, I couldn't stand it anymore, so I said again, "Look, I'm really, really sorry."

"Stop saying that!" he said angrily. I'm guessing he

didn't realize that some of my "sorrys" were dance-related.

"I can't. You're my best friend," I said, which sounded pathetic—I could tell from the look of discomfort on the other kids' faces. Chris was giving me a particularly weird look, which just made everything worse. *Stay out of it,* I thought angrily at Chris, even though he hadn't actually said anything.

"Just leave me alone," Dash hissed, and he stopped dancing and dropped my sleeve. Several kids crashed into each other as a result. ("Sorry!")

From across the room, Solly yelled, "Keep going, guys. And smile! This is Israeli dance, not the Middle East conflict! It's supposed to be fun!"

In retrospect, my mistake was probably that I stopped looking at my feet. That's why when I stepped on a banana peel—yes, the same one I tried unsuccessfully to toss in the trash and failed to pick up—I slipped and skidded right into Chris, totally by accident.

"Yo, man, watch out!" said Chris. We had reached the kicking part of the song, but instead of kicking the air, he aimed his foot and kicked me, like I had slid into him on purpose. I totally wanted to kick him back because I felt like, *Hey, this isn't my fault, you started it.* I resisted the impulse, but the whole thing got me really riled up, and when I went to clap, his face got in the way. Then Chris hit me back, and Dash started yelling, and suddenly Dash was on the ground. And then I jumped on Chris and hit him a bunch of times for, well, everything. I just couldn't help it. I hit him for being a jerk and stealing my best friend and all of it.

Some of the girls started shrieking and I could hear Noa yelling "Stop it, you guys! Stop it!" but other kids were yelling "Fight! Fight! Fight!" and before I knew what was happening Chris slammed my head on the ground and I tasted blood and carpet and then Solly and Rabbi Fred and Rabbi Jake were all there pulling me and Dash and Chris off each other.

They put me in the kitchen—probably because I was the only one bleeding and there's an ice machine there—and Chris and Dash in other places. Rabbi Fred stayed with me. He got me to sit with my head back and an ice pack on my nose. I tried to talk but he silenced me with a wave of his hand. "One thing at a time, Noah. For now, just count ceiling tiles, okay?"

I did as I was told. *Thirty-two.*

When they had cleared the social hall, they brought the three of us back there and sat us in chairs and made us all apologize. Then they lectured us for a while, and finally they had us call our parents for early pickup. I didn't get the chance to talk to Dash or explain, because his mom showed up first, and she took Chris home, too. Seeing the three of them leave together, like I used to do with Dash and his dad sometimes, made me feel like crying. Though it could have been that my nose still hurt like crazy.

Then I went upstairs with Rabbi Fred and sat with him in his office for a while.

"Is now a good time to talk?" I asked.

"Why don't we hold off until your moms get here? This seems like a conversation we should all have together."

I didn't like the sound of that, but I wasn't really in a position to argue. So Rabbi Fred worked at his desk. And I just sat there listening to the water feature flow and flow. After a while, he asked, "Guess your moms are stuck in traffic or something?"

I shrugged, then reached into my backpack to check my phone. When I pulled it out, something fell out of my bag. I realized what it was as it hit the floor: Dash's phone.

For a second, I thought maybe I could try to pass it off as my own phone. But I was already holding my own phone in my hand. And as it landed, screen-up, it lit up to show that there was an unread message:

Mom: Hi, Dashie. I'm assuming you got your phone back from Noah like you said you would. Meet you out front after Hebrew school. OK?

Rabbi Fred looked at the phone, then at me. I considered feigning total ignorance, or looking up at the ceiling, like Harpo Marx does in *Animal Crackers* when all the silverware is falling out of his sleeve. I even thought about saying something dumb, like I'd been framed or I had no idea what was going on. But my head hurt and there was blood in my mouth and I was tired of lying and fighting and pretending everything was okay.

"Oh, Noah," said Rabbi Fred. "Please don't tell me that's what I think it is."

Then he picked up Dash's phone.

"I'm sorry," I said in a little voice. I had never been this completely hopeless before. My plan to return Dash's phone and fix our friendship had failed. I had caused problems for so many people: Dash, Noa, Chris, Rabbi Fred. On top of that, my nose was maybe broken. It felt like everything good in my life was gone and I could never get it back. I wondered if this was how Gil had felt.

Fighting back tears, with a wad of paper towels under my nose in case it began to bleed again, I told Rabbi Fred what had happened. How I had found the phone and wanted to give it back to Dash immediately. But also how Dash was ignoring me and how I believed that if I looked at his texts, I could figure out a way to be a better friend to him. I explained that when I saw that he was mad at me and had a new best friend, it just made it more difficult to do what I knew was right. And that I'd listened to what he said about the sticks and the rocks and tried to do the right thing, only every time I tried, Dash wasn't there or he didn't want to talk to me, which made things harder.

"I know it probably sounds like I'm making excuses," I said. "I really didn't mean for things to get so messed up. I wanted to fix things. I just—" I stopped, at a loss for words. I looked at Rabbi Fred, hoping he would understand and tell me that it would be okay.

Rabbi Fred stared at me for a long time. Finally, he said, "Noah, there's something I hoped you would have figured out by now. But I suppose now is as good a time as any to learn it. I want to tell you a story, okay? It's about a young man who had a job after school, working in a bakery."

As he spoke, Rabbi Fred rummaged in his desk drawers and found some paper and a pack of markers. With a black marker, he drew a circle and put a dot at the center. As he added numbers along the outside edge, I realized that it was supposed to be a clock.

"So, this young man—I'll call him Ben—would arrive at the bakery every day at three o'clock in the afternoon." With the black marker, Rabbi Fred drew the clock's big hand, an arrow from the center dot pointing straight up at the number twelve. He then took a green marker and drew a smaller clock hand pointing at the number three. "The baker had to get up at the crack of dawn each day to bake the bread and open the bakery for the first customers. When Ben arrived, the two would talk for a few minutes, comparing notes, and then the baker would leave for the day. It was Ben's job to sell breads and pastries, make change, wipe the counters, sweep the floor, and close the store for the night at eight." Rabbi Fred took a red marker and drew another small clock hand arrow, this one pointing to the eight.

"It was a small shop, so every day between the hours of three and eight p.m., Ben was the only one working there. But one evening, at closing time, a woman with a little girl entered the shop. It was a cold night, but the child had no coat and the woman's dress was torn. The woman asked Ben if she could have a challah roll, and when Ben went to ring it up, she admitted she had no money and turned to leave. 'Just take it,' said Ben. Then he filled a bag with bread and gave that to her, too."

"That was nice of him," I said, dabbing at my nose.

Rabbi Fred continued his story. "The next day, one of Ben's friends from school came into the shop around five o'clock." He took an orange pen and drew another clock hand, this one pointing to the five. "Ben's friend wanted a pastry but had forgotten his wallet. Ben said, 'This one's on the house.' And the following day, around six o'clock, Ben's stomach started to growl." Rabbi Fred added another clock hand, this one a blue arrow pointing to the six. "Ben had missed lunch, and closing time seemed a long way off. Unable to wait, he took a muffin from the display case. It was so delicious he had another one, too.

"The following day, at five o'clock, Ben's friend stopped by again. Once again, he had forgotten his wallet. Ben scolded his friend, but he gave him a sweet anyway. At six o'clock, Ben got hungry again and took something from the case to silence his growling stomach. And at eight o'clock, the woman in the torn dress returned and Ben gave her food." Rabbi Fred used a marker to point to the times as he mentioned them, leaving small dots next to the five, six, and eight.

"This pattern repeated every day for one week, then two. Finally, Ben's boss, the baker, called him in. 'We have a problem,' he said. 'And it has been happening at the exact same time every day for two weeks.' What do you think the baker said next?"

" 'You're fired'?"

"Well, that's what you would think, right? But instead, the baker said, 'I am not going to fire you if you can tell me what time I'm talking about.' "

"Five o'clock?" I tried. I figured that giving food away to a friend was worse than giving it to a poor person or grabbing a snack while working. I wasn't sure where Rabbi Fred was going with this. I never gave away snack-table items. I hadn't even worked the snack table since the day he and I took a walk.

"Guess again."

"Six?"

"Nope."

"It couldn't be eight o'clock," I said, thinking out loud, "because giving food away to a poor person at closing time isn't bad, is it?"

"Any other guesses?" asked Rabbi Fred.

"Not really. Three o'clock is the only other time you mentioned."

"Correct."

"I give up," I said.

"You can't give up. You just solved it."

"Three o'clock? That doesn't make sense." I pointed at the clock drawing with the rainbow of hands and dots. "He never took anything at three."

"You're right," said Rabbi Fred. "But here's the thing. At three o'clock each day he would see the baker, his boss. So every day at three o'clock he had the opportunity to explain, or apologize, or offer to pay the baker back. Instead, what did he do?"

"Nothing," I said quietly.

Rabbi Fred nodded. "And that, according to the baker, was the bigger problem."

"Oh."

Rabbi Fred stood up. He took Dash's phone and left me alone in his office.

I looked at the clock drawing. Then I looked at the books on Rabbi Fred's shelves. They all seemed to be judging and accusing me. *Theories on Evil,* read one. *Little Failure,* another read. *Too Late for Redemption?* read a third. Sure, the title was stated as a question, but I was pretty sure I knew the answer. Rabbi Fred had just told me.

I waited for him to return with my moms so we could have the awful conversation we had to have together, which I was pretty sure would involve everyone getting mad at me. Maybe even Rabbi Fred, who never raised his voice. I closed my eyes.

The water ran and ran.

Other than that, the silence was deafening. *Maybe that is what the song means,* I realized. Maybe silence has a sound that you can only hear when it's so painful to be alone that you'd be grateful for anything that might chase it away.

Even yelling.

Chapter Twelve

A lot of things happened in the days that followed.

Not good things. Bad things.

For example, I had to write a lot of notes.

Like this one:

Dear Grandma Beth,

I hope you are doing well. I am writing to tell you that my bar mitzvah will not be taking place on April 30. I know that date has been on your calendar for a long time, and I know you were planning to come. The good news is that I will be having a bar mitzvah! I'm just not sure when. It's a long story.

I will let you know my new date when

they tell me. Give my love to Grandpa Joe when you visit him.

Sorry and please don't be mad.

Love,
Noah

I also had to write to the caterers, and the DJ (who, luckily, was a friend of Enid's), explaining what had happened and asking if they could please consider refunding our deposit. And at Rabbi Fred's "strong suggestion," I wrote a letter to my moms apologizing for letting them down.

The letter writing was one of the consequences imposed on me. The other was what the letters were about. It might sound dumb after the Israeli dance fight and Rabbi Fred discovering that I had Dash's phone, but I have to admit that I didn't see it coming. I had never heard of that happening to anyone before. I had thought I'd be a Hebrew school legend for inventing the Kings and Queens of Comedy Cabaret. Instead, I would probably go down in Hebrew school history for being the first kid ever to have his bar mitzvah revoked.

It happened like this. After Rabbi Fred left me alone in his office, he returned with both my moms, plus Rabbi Jake and Phyllis. They all looked very serious, like they'd already been talking about me.

Rabbi Fred led off by saying, "Up until this year, Noah's behavior at Hebrew school has never been a major problem. Perhaps he hasn't always been a model student at all times, but he's certainly never done anything that would cause us to question his character or his commitment." He mentioned the Israeli dance fight and having to speak with me repeatedly about my attitude toward Noa, but he mostly focused on the situation with Dash's phone. He reviewed the facts as he understood them:

1. I knew the phone I found was Dash's.
2. I did not return it or turn it in, even though I knew (because Rabbi Fred told me) that it had been reported missing.
3. Instead, I read his private messages.
4. And I lied, claiming I did not know of the phone's whereabouts.
5. Then I showed Dash that I had the phone, but did not return it to him.
6. And the rabbis only discovered that I had it when it fell out of my backpack in Rabbi Fred's office.

As Rabbi Fred ticked off my misdeeds on his fingers and calmly explained how I had violated a variety of our temple's written rules—as well as unwritten expectations—something dawned on me. Dash knew I had the phone, yet he didn't rat me out to the rabbis. And his mom's text suggested he'd told her I had it and that he was going to get it back from me. Was he planning to talk to me? Was there hope for our friendship after all?

My thoughts were interrupted by the sound of my moms responding to Rabbi Fred.

"I'm not defending Noah's behavior," said Karen. "But as I'm sure you're aware, this has been a rough year for him."

Jenny chimed in. "Dash and Noah have been close friends for years, and Noah used to sleep over at Gil's house all the time. And on top of Gil's death, it seems to Karen and me that things have been a little rocky between the boys lately."

"We've noticed that here, too," said Rabbi Jake, like I wasn't even there. "And we've certainly taken that into consideration and, at times, cut him some slack."

"The thing is," said Rabbi Fred, "we make our b'nei mitzvah schedule very far in advance, in anticipation not only that the children will use the time to prepare, but also that they will become mature enough to take on the increased responsibilities. However—"

"Can I say something?" I asked.

"No," said both my moms at once. "Wait your turn," added Karen.

Rabbi Fred continued. "Occasionally, there is a child who demonstrates that he or she is simply not ready to be lifted up, as it were, as a bar or bat mitzvah. When this occurs, the rabbinical staff discusses the circumstances and tries to determine if extra time will benefit the child's emotional development and readiness. In light of Noah's behavior recently," he concluded, "we feel the best recourse may be to defer his bar mitzvah ceremony. We are confident that in six months to a year, he will rise to the challenges and demonstrate his readiness."

"Can I say something?" I repeated, even though now it definitely seemed like it was too late.

"Of course," said Rabbi Fred.

"Please don't take away my bar mitzvah," I said. I could feel the tears coming, so I struggled to get the words out before I completely lost it. "I found the phone—I didn't take it. I tried to give it back, honest! And I took good care of the phone while I had it. I charged it, and put it in our rice jar, and washed it so it wouldn't smell like pee."

"Wait, what?" said Jenny.

"The point is," I continued quickly, "I'm really, really sorry."

Rabbi Fred spoke gently. "Listen, Noah," he said, "I know you've been working on your Torah portion and looking forward to celebrating with your family and friends. Just to be clear, we're making a decision not to take that opportunity away but to postpone it for the time being. All the same, I wouldn't blame you for feeling sad and frustrated and angry. I hope in the days to come you'll see that what we're actually doing is fulfilling our jobs as your teachers. In order to embrace you as a full member of our community, we need to believe you are ready."

"I am!" I said.

"I know that you want to be," he answered. "And that's a good thing. It means you're headed in the right direction."

The rabbis let us go home and said they would talk some more. But Rabbi Fred called the next day to tell my moms that they stood by their decision. Karen gave me the news, explaining that, according to the rabbis, the consequences needed to be major because I had broken several temple and Hebrew school rules, including fighting, taking something that didn't belong to me, lying about it, and violating the privacy of a classmate. The rabbis didn't specifically punish me for sending fake texts to Chris while pretending to be Dash, or for putting text swaps like "fartknocker," "armadillo butt," and "wiener" for "hi," "you," and "okay" in his phone. Possibly because they were already punishing me for the other reasons. Also because I'm not sure they were aware that I did this stuff.

There were other consequences that didn't come from the rabbis. Like Chris hating me. Not that we were ever friends, but we didn't cross over into being actual enemies until the whole Israeli dance war broke out. Now Chris and all the other seventh-grade boys who used to be my friends hated me.

Noa also hated me now. On top of all the seventh-grade boys hating me, the Israeli dance war translated into all the seventh-grade girls hating me, too. For all I knew, the fifth and sixth graders hated me as well, because they looked up to the seventh graders and tried to do whatever they did.

And, of course, Dash hated me most of all.

If anything was worse than that, it was probably knowing I let my moms down. The look on Karen's face when she got off the phone with Rabbi Fred made me sadder than anything I had ever experienced, except for Gil's death. Jenny seemed pretty upset, too, and she's not even Jewish. I thought about all the times my moms had driven me home from Hebrew school or gone to hear me sing in a special youth-choir service when I was little. Neither of them deserved this. They didn't mess things up. I did.

So I didn't argue when they decided to ground me for the rest of the school year. This meant that, except for Tuesdays when I still had Hebrew school, I had to come straight home. Which was sort of beside the point because I no longer had any friends. I mean, I still had my regular-school friends, but they were all busy with their own stuff and had no idea what I had been going through. Plus, the only friend that really mattered to me was Dash.

At that point, I was pretty sure things couldn't get any worse. So sure, in fact, I even perked up when I saw Dash and Noa coming my way during the snack break at Hebrew school.

"What's up?" I said. "You guys want to work on our Three Stooges presentation?" When the rabbis imposed their consequences, they did me exactly one favor by allowing me to satisfy my mitzvah project requirement with my class. In other words, they didn't make me sit out of the comedy cabaret and start a new project when and if they ever believed I was ready to become a bar mitzvah.

"Well, actually, that's what we wanted to talk to you about," said Dash, glancing nervously at Noa.

"Yes. We've discussed it and we've decided," she announced, "that it would be better for everyone if we didn't do the Three Stooges as our Kings and Queens of Comedy Cabaret project."

"Oh," I said. "What are we going to do instead?"

"We," said Noa firmly, "are going to do Jerry and Elaine from *Seinfeld.*"

"Oh," I said again. And then, to show I could be flexible, I offered, "Okay, I guess I could do George."

"Actually," said Noa, "you can do the Stooges by yourself if you want. Rabbi Jake said we don't have to work with you anymore." And with that, she led Dash away.

"You can't fire me. I quit!" I called after them. That was for Dash. It's what Latka said to Louie on *Taxi* in a scene Gil had shown us during SND. Dash was supposed to respond with "You're fired, you're fired, you're fired," fast and loud like Louie. And then I'd say "I quit, I quit, I quit" even faster.

But Dash didn't say anything. He didn't even turn around.

"Plus, I can't do the Stooges by myself!" I added, acutely aware that I sounded more than a little unhinged. "There are three of them. Four if you count Shemp. Which I don't!"

I can't even do George by myself, I thought miserably. *George is nothing without Jerry. Everybody knows that.*

Chapter Thirteen

Because Karen and Jenny were still so disappointed in me for losing my bar mitzvah, I decided not to mention that, on top of that, I had been kicked off my comedy cabaret team. It was one thing to keep something off my moms' radar. But Enid was another matter. So I was not surprised to find her at my bedroom door within hours of my getting unceremoniously de-Stooged.

"How's the comedy project going?" she asked.

"Wow, news travels fast," I said.

"What news?" she said. "I was just asking."

I groaned. "I don't have a comedy project," I admitted. "But you can't tell them." Meaning: our moms.

"I thought you were working with Dash and Noa, and doing the Three Stooges?" she said.

"I was. Past tense. I am an ex-Stooge."

"They're doing the Three Stooges without you?"

"No. They're doing Jerry and Elaine without me."

"So . . . you can still do the Stooges," suggested Enid.

"I don't want to do the Stooges by myself," I said. I didn't mean to sound whiny, but I couldn't help it. "There are three of them. Four if you count Shemp, which I don't, but there's never just one. But no one wants to work with me and it doesn't really matter anyway because they're not letting me have a bar mitzvah this year and maybe not ever."

"Whoa, whoa, whoa," said Enid. "Hang on a second. First of all, the whole comedy cabaret thing was your idea, right?"

I shrugged. I didn't know how to explain to her that that was *before.* Before Gil died. Before Dash stopped speaking to me. Before the Israeli dance war. Before I messed everything up and lost my bar mitzvah date and all my friends and everything that mattered.

"And you love this stuff, right? So why drop out when you can just go back to the drawing board and pick someone else?"

I thought for a moment. "I don't know," I finally said. "I have a lot of favorites."

"Okay, how about this. What if instead of just focusing on one comedian, you pulled together a reel of the best Jewish comedy clips?"

"I dunno," I said reluctantly.

Enid raised an eyebrow. "It's your call," she said.

"But if you did go that route, who would you want to include?"

"The Three Stooges, Jerry Seinfeld, the Marx Brothers, Billy Crystal, Woody Allen . . ." My mind started racing with the possibilities. "Gene Wilder and Gilda Radner. Oh, and Rachel Bloom, she's hilarious. You know, *Crazy Ex-Girlfriend*?" It was like creating a fantasy sports roster, which was something some of the guys at school loved but I never saw the point of. However, a fantasy *comedy* roster—a sort of Jewish comedy all-stars—now that was something I could wrap my head around.

"What about Joan Rivers?" suggested Enid.

"What about her?"

"She's really funny. Plus, she's incredibly brave. Get this: her husband committed suicide. Most people wouldn't be able to find humor in that, but she did, and she kind of made history by doing so. Hang on, I'll show you."

Enid dug around on the Internet for a while. Finally, she came up with a clip from an interview in which Joan Rivers talked about how hard it was after her husband died and how it still affected her, like when their daughter got married and he wasn't there to walk her down the aisle. That made me think of Noa and Dash, who wouldn't have their dads at their bar and bat mitzvahs.

But then Joan Rivers explained how she pushed herself to use her pain to find humor. Making fun of herself for being addicted to shopping at a certain fancy store, she told a joke: "My husband killed himself and left a message that I have to visit him every day, so I had him cremated and sprinkled him in Neiman Marcus. Haven't missed a day."

I couldn't help it: I laughed. For the first time in a long time.

"Wow. You think I can use it?" I asked Enid.

"Maybe," she said. "Let's put it on the list for now."

We did some more searching and found more clips. We found Andy Kaufman doing Latka on *Taxi*. We pulled the one of Krusty the Clown's bar mitzvah. And we pulled another one of the son on the show *Black-ish* declaring that he wanted a bar mitzvah, too, even though he wasn't Jewish. I was torn about including that one because the only Jewish comedian in the scene, Tracee Ellis Ross, had practically no lines, but Enid encouraged me to collect everything and edit later.

Enid and I watched a bunch of Mel Brooks movie clips before deciding which one to go with. I had to admit the project was really taking shape. I only wished that Dash, and even annoying old Noa, were there to work on it with me, too. As fun as it was to get to be in charge and make all the decisions, it wasn't anywhere near as fun as watching and selecting clips with my friends would've been.

Finally, after making several difficult cuts (sorry, Tracee!), I ran the compilation of clips in sequence. It was really funny and really good. We even found a way to put Monty Python in it—their lack of Jewishness notwithstanding—by using a "Nobody Expects the Spanish Inquisition" clip, which felt like a nice homage to Dash's dad. I felt really good and proud and was sort of sad to be seeing the project come to an end. Or almost an end, because I still needed to figure out which comedian to be if I ended up going to the cabaret after all.

That night, Enid knocked on my door, carrying Raspberry. "Hey," she said, "I found something you need to see."

"What is it?" I asked.

She didn't answer. Instead, she just said, "Come with me."

When we got to the computer, she pulled up the clip. It was on YouTube, but it was on a page I hadn't seen before. It had a whole bunch of videos, all of which appeared to have been privately posted.

"What are these?" I asked.

"They're Jenny's home movies from when we were little," Enid told me, scrolling down through them until she found the one she was looking for. She clicked on it and I saw Enid, only much younger, standing in our living room holding a big flowered bag. She was checking the pretend watch on her wrist and looking to one side like she was waiting for a bus.

"Wait a second, is this—" But before I could ask, a younger version of myself walks across the screen wearing a T-shirt, shorts, and a huge sombrero hat. And little Enid stops checking her wrist, stares at the hat, and says her line: "Nice hat! Where'd you get it?"

"Mistuh Maxx," little-kid me tells her.

" 'Mr. Maxx'?" I said. "This is us doing the skit?"

"Yup," said Enid. "But it gets better. Wait for it."

Next Dash walks across the living room. He is wearing a pair of shoes that probably belonged to his dad, so he walks with exaggerated *clomp-clomp-clomps*. Enid tells him that she loves his shoes, and Dash delivers his line—"Mr. Maxx!"—and exits. Then I come through again, wearing a Hawaiian shirt. Then Dash again, wearing a scuba mask and snorkel. "Mr. Maxx."

I was expecting to see Pete make his diapered entrance, as this was our usual finale. So I was surprised by what came next.

Dash's dad, in his running clothes and with a bath towel tied around his midsection, appears on the screen. It was bizarre to see him, not just because he looked so much younger but also because he was playing a part that I didn't recall him ever playing. Was he some sort of understudy for Pete? He looked sweaty, so maybe we'd recruited him at the last minute that day because Pete had a meltdown or was taking a nap or something. Gil is wearing glasses I didn't remember and has a lot more hair on his head, but his gorilla arms are unmistakable. I realized I was already forgetting so much about his face and the way he moved. It made me sad to see him, but in another way it also made me really happy, like if he had gone away on a long trip but had finally returned.

"Who are you?" asks little Enid on the screen. I guess because Pete was not playing his usual role, the situation had thrown her timing off a bit.

"That's what I keep asking myself," says Gil, a strange, uncomfortable laugh catching in his throat. And I had never noticed the wistful note to his voice before.

The other thing I noticed was Dash standing at the side of our "stage," almost out of the frame, watching his dad. He seems really nervous, shifting his weight from side to side like maybe he has to pee. But also it seems a little like he is the dad who is watching his kid onstage instead of vice versa. He looks like he is standing ready because at any moment he might need to run on and rescue Gil. Like Chopper 4 or something.

It made me think of the thing Dash said when he bailed on having a sleepover that weekend before Gil died: *My dad needs me here.* Did Dash know his dad was in pain, even when we were little, even though no one else could see? Did Dash feel responsible for taking care of Gil? Except for once when Karen and Jenny both had the stomach flu at the same time, I couldn't think of any times I'd ever felt like my moms needed me to take care of them instead of the other way around. And even then, there was Enid, plus Grandma Beth came and helped out.

"Look. I'm totally freaking out," said Enid, pointing

to herself in the center of the frame. "I knew I blew my big line."

"Oh?" says little Enid, looking desperate to save the day. "Where are all your clothes?"

"My clothes?" Gil looks down and reacts like he is just noticing for the first time that he is only wearing a towel. We must have hoped our audience wouldn't notice that he actually had clothes on underneath it. "Oh. Sorry! I'm Mr. Maxx!"

At which point Dash and I run out giggling to take our bows, then practically attack Jenny, howling that we need to see the movie right now! But she shoos us away and keeps filming, so we got to see Gil trying to keep his towel from falling off while he takes a bow with Enid. The whole time, Gil has this big goofy grin on his face, which is how I remembered him. But watching it now, I was struck by how hard it looked like he was working to keep that smile on. Almost as hard as he was working to keep that towel from falling off—which it did when Dash and I started pulling on it.

"Was Gil always like that?" I asked Enid.

"What, depressed?" she asked.

I nodded, relieved to have her say what I was thinking.

"Kinda," she admitted. "I mean, I didn't know him like you did. But I definitely remember him being like that a lot." She gestured toward the screen for emphasis.

"Can we watch it again?"

And we did. Three more times, actually. And the last time we even stopped it at the moment when Gil says, "That's what I keep asking myself."

"Why didn't anyone do anything?" I asked her.

"What, to help him? I'm sure they did. I mean, it was a long time ago, but I know Stacey definitely talked to the moms about getting him some help."

"But it wasn't enough," I said. "I mean, obviously. They should have tried something else."

"Like what?" asked Enid.

"I don't know," I admitted. "Something so he'd still be here."

"I wish it worked that way, kiddo," said Enid. "But it doesn't."

"How do you know?" I asked her.

"We bats are very observant," said Enid quietly. She kept on petting Raspberry, who narrowed her green eyes down to slits as if to say to me, *Don't push it.*

So I didn't. Instead, I reached out and petted Raspberry, too. For once, to her credit, the World's Most Aloof Cat generously accepted my affection.

Chapter Fourteen

I got Enid to send me the link to the "Mr. Maxx" video and I watched it a bunch more times on my phone. I liked it for lots of reasons. It was like having a little memento, a reminder of Gil I could carry in my pocket. I marveled at how an old movie could show me something I couldn't see with my own eyes. Plus, it was funny. Maybe not funny in the way we meant it to be. But funny in a different way: sweet and sort of lumpy, like those Bartons Almond Kisses that Grandma Beth keeps in a tin in her kitchen. It wasn't Kings and Queens of Comedy Cabaret material, but it was definitely something special. More than anything, I wanted to share it with the one person other than me who would recognize its significance: Dash.

"So show it to him." That was Enid's answer when I

asked for her advice. She didn't even look up from the book she was reading.

"But he's still not speaking to me," I said.

Enid closed the book around a finger to hold her place and looked up at me. "Maybe he will if you show him the video," she suggested. "After all, it ended up in your hands for a reason, don't you think?"

"It ended up in my hands because you showed it to me," I reminded her.

"Yeah, but think about it," said Enid. "Why did I happen to find it when I did? I'd never seen it before. Doesn't it feel like some sort of unseen forces were potentially involved?"

"Like what? God?" I laughed nervously.

Enid shrugged. "I don't really do organized religion," she said. "But you do, so you tell me."

"I mean, maybe," I said, mulling it over. Maybe Enid was onto something. Maybe God had sent me the video as a way to connect with Dash again. Not exactly a do-over, but sort of the next best thing. I definitely liked the sound of that. But based on my recent experiences with Dash, I was wary, too.

"What if it's not, though?" I asked. "What if instead it makes him even madder at me than he already is? Maybe he doesn't want to see some dumb old video that reminds him of his dad."

"You got me," said Enid, reopening her book to signal that, as far as she was concerned, the conversation was over.

But before I left, I asked her one more thing. "What would you do if it were you?"

"If what were me?"

"I mean, let's say you found something you wanted to show your mom, but you weren't sure if she'd like it or if it would upset her. Like maybe something having to do with Howard. What would you do?"

Enid didn't close the book again, but she did stop reading long enough to consider this. Finally, she said, "I guess I might ask Karen. You know, because she could probably guess how my mom might react. Since she knows her best. I mean, next to me."

"Thanks!" I told her. And I meant it. Because I suddenly had my answer, and it made perfect sense. According to Enid, I needed to show the video to the person Dash felt closest to right now. The one he trusted with his deepest, darkest secrets. That person could help me decide if, when, and how I should show the video to Dash.

In other words, I needed to show it to Chris.

The next Tuesday afternoon, there was no Hebrew school because later that evening we were holding our big community event, the Kings and Queens of Comedy Cabaret.

After much agonizing, I had put together a costume. And my moms had agreed to contribute food, so we arrived early to set up, and I changed in the boys' room.

Walking upstairs, I practically collided with Groucho Marx.

"Sorry!"

In the main lobby, I saw Groucho Marx again, only this one was much taller. Then I saw Groucho Marx in braids, and Groucho Marx with braces, and Groucho Marx in wheelies. At first it seemed like the setup for a joke ("Five Grouchos walk into a bar . . ."). But then I noticed that next to the usual bowl of spare yarmulkes, there was an even bigger bowl of Groucho Marx nose-and-mustache glasses and a sign that said GROUCHO YOURSELF! Apparently, anyone in our class who didn't wear a costume, as well as anyone attending the community event, could be an honorary Groucho for the night.

I was briefly tempted to ditch my costume and go the Groucho route myself. But before I could do so, Dash and Noa walked in together wearing their Jerry and Elaine costumes. Dash was wearing a white shirt with rows of ruffles, just like in the "Puffy Shirt" episode of *Seinfeld,* and he was carrying a take-out coffee cup in one hand and a box of Junior Mints in the other. Noa was wearing a dark brown wig with glasses perched on the top of it, plus a suit jacket, a long flowered skirt, and lace-up boots with white socks.

I was staring at them, trying to think of something clever to say, when Noa marched over to me and asked, "What are you supposed to be?"

The sting of seeing Noa and Dash doing their team costume together without me was more than I had planned on, but there was no turning back now. "Guess," I said to Noa, pretending to play it cool as Dash went to talk to a bunch of Grouchos in the corner.

Noa looked me up and down. "I don't know," she finally said. "You look like an explosion in a costume shop."

She wasn't too far off, since I was wearing a bald cap and a curly wig and a black bowl-cut wig all at once.

"I'm the Three Stooges," I told her.

"Oh!" she said, surprised. "I thought you were—"

"*All* three Stooges," I announced. Then I stormed off, removed the two wigs, and found a place to sulk behind a potted plant. I found a broken, mustacheless pair of Groucho Marx glasses back there, so I put them on and hid behind them for the rest of the evening. I really wanted to go home, but I hung in there and reminded myself that, like Enid said, the whole thing had been my idea in the first place and I loved this stuff. Plus, I still wanted to talk to Chris like I'd planned.

Unsurprisingly, Chris was one of the Grouchos. I mean, sure, I was a Groucho now, too, but at least I came to the event in costume. Heck, I came in three costumes! It killed me that Dash had replaced me with a best friend so lacking in creativity that he didn't even try to make a costume of his own. But that wasn't the point, I reminded myself. Dash trusted Chris, so surely there was a reason they were close. Whether I could see it or not, there had to be something special about Chris.

The first half of the program went pretty well. Rabbi Jake took the stage as the Kings and Queens of Comedy Cabaret master of ceremonies, and he actually gave me a shout-out for being the one who came up with the idea. Noa and Dash did their Jerry and Elaine presentation and skit, and Noa was surprisingly funny. She even did the Elaine dance, which took guts. She looked a little bit like Jenny does when Karen pulls her out on the dance floor. Maya did a tribute to Sarah Silverman, and Rabbi Jake only had to interrupt twice to remind her that there were small children in the audience. And Adam, Jared, Sarah, and Sadie closed out the first half with the stateroom scene from the Marx Brothers' *Night at the Opera.* I found it confusing that all four of them were wearing Groucho glasses, but the resounding applause suggested I was alone in that view.

During the intermission, I asked Chris if I could talk to him. I actually asked one of the other Grouchos first, but once I realized I had the wrong one, he pointed out the right Groucho to me (Groucho in a Nats jersey, not a Wizards jersey).

Chris followed me into the library, where I gave him a bit of background information before pulling out my phone, finding the "Mr. Maxx" video, and hitting play. We probably looked a little silly: two Grouchos, one bald and mustacheless, the other in a baseball jersey, hunched over a phone screen.

"What is this?" said Chris.

I took a deep breath, pressed pause, and explained again. "Like I said before, it's a video Dash and I made when we were little. It's a comedy routine, okay? That's my sister." I pointed to Enid, who was on the screen checking her fake watch and waiting for her fake bus. "And later you'll see Dash's dad."

"Why are you showing me this?" said Chris. Honestly, I was more confused than ever about why he was now Dash's best friend. Not only was he failing to see the humor in the obviously funny setup, he seemed even more insensitive than, well, me.

I tried again. "I'm thinking that maybe it's going to be hard for Dash to see a video that has his dad in it. Especially when his dad seems so, I dunno, depressed in it. Wait, you'll understand in a minute." I waited for the part where Dash's dad says, "That's what I keep asking myself."

When it came, I paused the video again. "See what I mean?" I asked. "Do you think it'll upset him to see this? Or do you think he'd want to see it?"

"I don't know," said Chris. "Why are you asking me?"

"Because you're his best friend," I said.

"No, I'm not," said Chris.

I stared at him. I wasn't sure why both of them were trying to keep their friendship such a big secret. Maybe because Chris didn't know I'd read his texts and I knew about Dash's dad. I decided it was time to come clean. "Look, Chris, I know," I said.

"Know what?"

"About you and Dash."

"What about me and Dash?" said Chris. He sounded irritated, like I was suggesting they were dating or something.

"I read your texts on Dash's phone," I admitted. "I know Dash told you about his dad committing suicide."

"His dad doing what?" yelled Chris, looking horrified.

"You already know that," I said patiently.

"Dude, you're crazy," said Chris. At this point, Rabbi Jake was standing at the library door. He was dressed in a leather jacket with his hair slicked back like the Fonz, I guess because Henry Winkler is Jewish. It seemed like a reach to me because it's not like he's a comedian per se, unless you count his role on *Arrested Development*, but I wasn't about to point this out to him at that particular moment.

"Um, Groucho? George? What's going on?" asked Rabbi Jake.

"Nothing," I said, shoving my phone in my pocket and trying not to be irritated that he mistook me for George Costanza. Chris ran out, pushing past Rabbi Fonzie.

Chris's reaction made no sense. It was one thing for

him to deny knowing things he didn't know I knew he knew. But to call me crazy and act like he was going to catch my crazy if he stood too close to me? That was just plain weird. It made me think of the scene from *Young Frankenstein* I had put in my video montage. It was the one where the mad scientist, played by Gene Wilder, asks his assistant, Igor, whose brain they put in the monster. "Abby . . . someone," says Igor. "Abby . . . Normal." Maybe there was something seriously abby-normal, I mean abnormal, about Chris. Like received-the-wrong-brain weird.

If Dash ever started talking to me again, I'd need to mention this to him. Of course, it was only a matter of time before Dash found out. Not about Chris's brain transplant. About what I said to Chris.

It happened during the second half of the program. I was scheduled to go first. Rabbi Jake introduced me and I did a little stand-up, then showed my comedy clip montage. I sat on a wooden stool at the side of the stage, watching the audience watch the videos, which was the part I was really looking forward to. I figured it would be a little like SND, watching everyone laugh at the clips I chose. Instead, I watched in horror as Groucho whispered to Groucho, who whispered to Groucho, who then whispered to all the other Grouchos. The fact that all the parents, standing at the back, were guffawing appreciatively at my clips could not distract me from noticing that my conversation with

Chris was going viral. It reminded me of the time Rabbi Jake gave a sermon about social media and told a story about a man trying to put feathers back into a pillow with a rip in it. Trapped onstage, I watched in horror as feathers fluttered in all directions. Sooner or later one of them was likely to land on Dash. Probably sooner.

Much sooner, it turned out. The minute I stepped off-stage, Jerry Seinfeld—or rather, Dash—marched over to me and said the words I had been waiting for him to say. Just not in the way I hoped he would say them.

"I need to talk to you."

"Okay," I said, and followed him to the boys' room.

Dash checked under the stall doors to make sure we were alone, then wasted no time getting to the point. "Why are you spreading rumors about my dad?" he demanded.

"I'm not," I said truthfully.

"Oh yeah?" said Dash. "Well, then why is everyone talking about my dad killing himself? Chris Stern says you started it."

"I didn't tell him that," I reminded him. "*You* did."

"What are you talking about?! I didn't tell him that! I've only told one person about my dad and it definitely *wasn't* Chris Stern."

"Yes, you did!" I insisted. "You texted him about it, and I saw it because I had your phone."

"I did not!" he yelled. He was turning kind of red and indignant, so I really just wanted to get him to calm down so one of the rabbis—or worse, Phyllis—wouldn't come running in. So I tried to walk him through it slowly.

"Look," I said, "I know I shouldn't have kept your phone or read your texts. That wasn't okay and I wanted to give it back and apologize for a long time. But the thing is, I saw what you told Chris. I saw the whole long conversation on your phone."

"What," demanded Dash, "did you see?"

"You told him, and I quote, that you 'kind of' hated me," I said. "And then I wrote back as you—which, yes, I know I shouldn't have done—and asked him why. And Chris got confused and thought you were talking about what your dad did. That's how I knew you told him what your dad did."

"I didn't tell you *or* Chris Stern," insisted Dash.

There was something about his insistence that was starting to unhinge me. "If you don't believe me," I said, "look for yourself. It's right there in your message history. You and CS."

"CS?" said Dash.

And then I had an awful feeling.

"Yes," I said. "CS is Chris Stern, right?"

"Wrong," said Dash. Then he stormed out of the boys' room.

The next Tuesday, everyone at Hebrew school couldn't stop talking about the cabaret. Our grade was getting tons of props for coming up with such a cool and innovative idea for a community event, and for raising so much money, all of which would go to charity. I would have loved to bask in the glory, except I couldn't. I had lost enthusiasm for everything I once cared about, especially comedy. And all I could remember about the night was the nauseating sensation of standing onstage watching the Groucho gossip chain and realizing that I had destroyed my last chance of reconnecting with Dash.

The rabbis had sent out an email congratulating all the seventh graders, and also reminding everyone to bring their Groucho glasses back so the synagogue could hang on to them for another comedy cabaret, or some other future event. I was guessing they might be figuring out how to work Groucho into their Purim spiel. So I ended up with the honor of collecting all the leftover Groucho glasses to return to Rabbi Fred for safekeeping.

Wearing a pair of Groucho glasses and taking my time—if I finished early, I'd just end up in Israeli dance or worse—I trudged from classroom to classroom, gathering the rest of the pairs in a plastic storage bin. Several were in sorry shape, with earpieces dangling off, mushed noses, or missing mustaches. They reminded me of how, in the movie *Take the Money and Run,* Woody Allen keeps getting his glasses taken off and stomped on, again and again and again. *I can relate, Woody,* I thought. Even though, in my case, I seemed to be the one stepping on my own glasses repeatedly.

When I had visited all the classrooms, I went to deliver the glasses to Rabbi Fred.

"Hiya, Groucho," he said as I entered his office. "You can put them on the table, thanks."

I did as he asked, setting them down next to the water feature, which was flowing and flowing, as always.

" 'Water is water,' " I blurted out.

"Sorry?"

I took off my Groucho glasses and gestured with them to the faucet before adding them to the collection. " 'Art is art. . . . Water is water.' Groucho Marx was actually the one who said that."

"Really?" said Rabbi Fred.

"Uh-huh, in *Animal Crackers,*" I told him. "You can look it up."

"I believe you," said Rabbi Fred.

"Are you going to add it to the list?" I asked.

"Nope. The list is strictly for what my students think."

"Oh," I said, heading for the door. "I guess I'm not your student anymore."

Rabbi Fred stopped me. "Groucho Marx, may he rest in peace, is not my student," he said. "But of course you are, Noah. Why would you say that?"

"I dunno. I figured I might get assigned to a different tutor," I said. "I mean, who knows when my bar mitzvah will be? If I even end up having one. After, you know, everything. Instead of becoming a man, I kind of became an—" I caught myself in time and switched to "jerk."

"Noah, sit down for a minute. I think I need to clear up a few things." I sat across from him, and he looked me in the eye. "First, making some poor choices—even a *lot* of poor choices—does not mean you're a *jerk*," said Rabbi Fred. "Second, I'll let you in on a little secret. According to Jewish law, you do not need to be called to the Torah and chant and receive blessings to become a bar or bat mitzvah."

"You don't?"

Rabbi Fred shook his head.

"Then why are we expected to do those things?"

"I guess God loves a good chocolate fountain as much as the rest of us," said Rabbi Fred. "I'm kidding!" he quickly added. "There are lots of good reasons we ask our twelve- and thirteen-year-olds to dedicate themselves to their studies and demonstrate a certain level of maturity before we are willing to hold them up and invite our community to celebrate their coming-of-age. But, like I said, there's truly no magic about standing on the bimah. However, I'd appreciate it if you didn't go spreading this around."

"You're thinking we kids will revolt?"

"Actually, it's the parents I'm more worried about," said Rabbi Fred. "But here's the most important thing. The goal of the b'nei mitzvah year is not for you to become a man or a woman."

"It's not?"

"Nope. The goal, in fact, is the same as it is every year from the day you were born until you are as old as, well, I am." He laughed. "Or, dare I say it, even older. You want to know what it is?"

I nodded.

"We want you to become responsible and mature, sure. We'd like you to become a contributing member of our community, absolutely. But our goal, above everything else, is that you become a mensch," he said.

"My moms say some people are mensches and some aren't," I told him. "You are," I added.

"Thanks," said Rabbi Fred. "With all due respect to your marvelous and menschy mothers, I have to disagree. Menschiness is something that must be cultivated. It's like music. Some people are fortunate enough to be born with phenomenal voices. But everyone—okay, almost everyone—has the potential, with some practice, to carry a tune. And everyone has the potential to be menschy."

That made me feel good. It gave me the confidence that even someone like me might actually get to that menschy place someday. I was grateful to Rabbi Fred for seeing that in me. It made me want to give back something to him, though I really didn't have anything to give. I was about to leave when that stupid faucet, running and running, caught my eye. And I noticed that sitting on top of the other rocks was the small reddish stone Rabbi Fred had picked up by the creek. It reminded me of a book I had when I was little about a donkey who wishes on a red pebble and turns himself into a big rock. The book scared me, even though it ended happily. I always made my moms skip the page where a wolf climbs on top of the rock and howls because he is cold. The noise I used to imagine him making was definitely a sound of silence.

"Do you want to know what I think?" I suddenly asked Rabbi Fred. "About the water?" For the first time ever, I knew what I thought about his question. And I needed to say it, even though I also knew it wasn't likely to earn me a Tootsie Pop.

"Very much," said Rabbi Fred.

"I think it's a lie."

Rabbi Fred looked at me with curiosity but not anger. "What's a lie?" he asked.

"The faucet. Water doesn't flow forever like that. Sometimes it runs out and that's it. Like we run out of hot water at my house all the time, especially when my sister takes long showers. And even though I know water's supposed to be a cycle, sometimes it rains for days, and other times it doesn't and my moms make me drag the hose out to water the plants. Sometimes gone is gone."

Rabbi Fred was quiet for a minute.

"I hope you're not mad that I called it a lie," I said.

"Not at all," said Rabbi Fred. "Actually, I thank you, Noah. You have given me something to study."

It wasn't until I got home that I realized there had been no Tootsie Pop. I hadn't made the list. Telling Rabbi Fred what I really thought about the water feature wasn't the same as making the list.

But in a funny way, it was better.

Chapter Fifteen

"I don't see why I can't wear my good sweatpants," I protested. "It's not like it's my bar mitzvah."

"It should have been," said Karen. Immediately she amended her comment with a "Sorry!"

"Let it go, Kar," said Jenny. Then she turned to me. "Noah, please do us all a favor and change your pants. We're late as it is. Besides, we're all going. So if I have to get dressed up, you do, too." If anyone hates wearing fancy clothes more than I do, it's probably Jenny.

"Noa doesn't care what we wear, really!" I objected, though I said it while stomping up to my room. To change my pants.

I really didn't want to go to Noa's bat mitzvah at all, but my moms said I had to. Since losing my bar mitzvah date, I had avoided the bar and bat mitzvahs of my classmates. However, Noa's mom and stepdad had invited my whole family to the party as well as the service, so it seemed there was no way to get out of it. I considered faking an illness, but since the unveiling, my moms had gotten wise to my ways. No, it was easier to just grin and bear it. Or at least just bear it.

When we got to the temple, I was actually glad my moms and Enid were there. Usually, all of us Hebrew school kids sit together, but since no one wanted to be my friend anymore, I knew better than to try and find a seat in that section. Many of them were wearing their tallises, signifying that they had already had their bar and bat mitzvahs, something I would not be able to do anytime soon. Instead, I sat up front with my family, which was good because it meant I didn't have to look at my classmates during the service. I did turn around in my seat at one point to look for Dash, and I saw some of Noa's friends from school arrive, whispering behind their programs and gazing with curiosity at the big wooden ark and the Ner Tamid hanging above it. If I had been ushing, I would have explained how the ark holds the Torah scrolls and that the Ner Tamid is a light that never goes out, not even in a power failure. But I wasn't asked to ush, so I just sat there silently. I didn't see Dash, which was sad but also a little bit of a relief.

When things got started, Noa came in and went up on the bimah with the rabbis and Phyllis. Noa was wearing a fancy dress and a rainbow tallit, as I predicted.

She looked nervous, which was surprising, considering how well prepared I knew she was.

After Phyllis led songs and the rabbis led prayers and all the preliminary parts of the service were done, Noa got up to do her *d'var Torah*. That's the part where you talk about what your Torah portion means and how it relates to contemporary life and beliefs. I had studied this particular parsha enough to have a good idea of what she'd be talking about. *Acharei Mot* has to do with what happens after the deaths of Aaron's two sons. God has killed them to punish them for breaking rules about when and how to enter the altar, and God goes on to spell out a whole bunch of rules for a community seeking forgiveness. Rabbi Fred told me and Noa that these rules went on to form the basis for Yom Kippur, which is the High Holiday we spend fasting and atoning for the sins of the previous year. So that's what I thought Noa was going to talk about. Rules, apologizing, making things right.

Instead, Noa got up and walked to the podium, and this is what she said:

"Hi. Today I will become a bat mitzvah, or daughter of the commandment. I stand before you to take part in this important tradition of our people. I am ready to read from the Torah, I am happy to tell you what it means to me, and I am honored to have this opportunity to take my place in our congregation.

"And, honestly, I am terrified.

"I know that's a strange thing to say. It's not because

I'm not ready to read the prayers, or chant from the Torah, or do any of the things that are expected of me. Because I am. I'm scared because I feel like my life is going really fast. I'm thirteen years old and it feels like yesterday I was at the playground digging in the sandbox. I'm afraid that if I blink, I'll find myself sixteen, then twenty-six, then forty-six—which my mom promises is not really old"—she got a laugh for that—"but you know what I mean.

"This has been on my mind a lot lately because my portion is called *Acharei Mot,* which means 'after the death.' As many of you know, I lost my father to cancer when I was just three years old. And I lost my grandpa more recently—last summer, in fact. And then, just a few months ago, a good friend of mine lost his dad, too. This friend of mine and I started texting, and then talking a lot about how hard this is, which has been a comfort to me and hopefully to him, too. Because whenever it's a big day for me, like a birthday or, well, today, I feel the loss all over again. I don't think that's ever going to go away."

I looked up, confused. I had read all of Dash's texts. There were none from Noa whatsoever. Lots of unanswered texts from other girls, and guys, and me. Tons of texts from CS and . . .

Then, all of a sudden, I got it.

CS.

Chris wasn't CS.

Noa was.

Up on the bimah, Noa continued. "But I realized something recently that has helped me a lot. I went to visit my dad, like I do sometimes. I picked up a rock to put on top of his headstone. And then when I put it there, I looked at the words. My dad's headstone has his full name, David Avram Cohen. Then it reads BELOVED HUSBAND AND FATHER, which he was. Underneath, it has the date he was born and the date he died. So his whole life—every hug, every push on the swings, every bedtime story—is represented by that little line connecting the two dates. Just that one little dash.

"Maybe that sounds depressing. But for me, it was just the opposite. It helped me see that life is what you make of it, and whether it is a long life or a short one matters less than how you live during the time you have.

"Another thing that made me realize this was some videos I watched with two of my classmates. Some of you might not know this, but this year our b'nei mitzvah class did a yearlong study of Jewish comedy as our mitzvah project. The culmination was a community event that we called the Kings and Queens of Comedy Cabaret. It was a big success, and our class has decided that all the money we raised will go to the Hope for Henry Foundation, which is a local organization that helps kids with life-threatening illnesses. 'Live well and laugh hard' is their motto, which fits perfectly with our theme.

"Anyway, when two of my friends and I were working on the mitzvah project, the first video they showed me was the Three Stooges. And I hated it. I'm sorry, I don't mean to be rude to anyone who loves the Three Stooges. I just couldn't understand how it could be funny for people to be hitting each other and pulling each other's ears and causing each other pain. But now I feel like I get it. Life is painful, but life is also funny. Sometimes at the same time. That's how we know we're alive. By crying, but also by laughing. It feels really good to laugh. My mom says I was too young to remember this, but I swear I can remember the sound of my dad's laugh.

"*Acharei Mot* is a Torah portion about the importance of seeking forgiveness, and the specific steps you need to take when you seek forgiveness. I think this is important, because none of us are above reproach. So I want to take this opportunity to say something that might come as a surprise to even my closest friends: I know I'm not perfect. None of us are. And from now on, I want to try to be a better friend, and a better daughter, and a better person. I want to make the most of my life. I want all of us to. Thank you."

I have never been to a bar or bat mitzvah service where people applauded at the end of the *d'var Torah.*

Until Noa's.

She got a freaking standing ovation, right there at temple. I don't even remember how the actual Torah part went, though I'm guessing she didn't mess up much, since that's just how she is. I was completely blown away by that speech she gave.

Afterward, all her friends rushed up to her in the hall and were hugging and kissing and high-fiving her. I hung back, almost afraid to get near her. Finally, I went over as she headed for the stairs to the reception, trailing an entourage of friends and family.

To my surprise, she gave me a big hug. "Hey, thanks so much for coming, Noah," she said.

"Oh! Sure," I said, trying to act like I hug girls I'm not related to all the time. "Good job."

"Thanks!" she said, breaking into a grin. "Whew! I was really nervous." And then she added, "I'm sorry about everything that happened. I wish you could've been up there with me."

"Me too," I told her. And I was surprised to realize that I actually meant it. Not just the having-my-bar-mitzvah part. Everything, even with Noa. Especially with Noa. I thought about what she said about Dash and almost asked why he wasn't there. *Quick, change the subject,* I told myself. "Uh, maybe I can hire you to do the speech at mine," I joked. "You killed."

Noa looked really pleased by my compliment. And even though I said "killed," which was kind of an unfortunate choice of words, she didn't wince or yell at me or anything. Instead, she said, "Are you coming down to the social hall for the party?"

"Sure, I'll be there in a minute."

I had seen Rabbi Fred head for his office and decided to go thank him for the pep talk he'd given me. I was about to knock on his door when I noticed something new. A little doorbell had been installed right next to the door. A handwritten sign read GIVE ME A RING, so I did.

"Come in," said Rabbi Fred. Kind of classic that he stopped saying "You rang?" as soon as he got a doorbell.

"I just stopped by to tell you— Hey," I interrupted myself. "Where's your water feature?"

"You know, Noah, I recently decided to switch up my decor. And I have you to thank."

"You do?"

Rabbi Fred nodded. "Yes. For helping me become aware that what I always saw as a positive symbol might be sending the opposite message to some of my students."

"I mean, maybe just one of them," I said apologetically. "Everybody else seemed to like it."

"It's okay," said Rabbi Fred. "Change is good." I must have looked unconvinced, because he quickly added, "Look at the evidence. You've got to admit that my decor change is good."

I couldn't argue with him there. He had several new items on display, including a big green-and-yellow lava lamp and a smaller round item that looked really familiar.

"You got a Magic 8 Ball?" I asked.

Rabbi Fred grinned and tossed it to me. "Nope!" he said proudly. "It's a Jewish Wisdom Ball."

I turned the ball over in my hands. It felt just like a Magic 8 Ball, but instead of the number eight, it had two Hebrew letters on it: *chet* and *yod*. Together, they spelled the word *chai*. Even with my limited Hebrew skills, I knew that means "life," like what people say when they clink their glasses at weddings: "*L'chaim!* To life!"

"But it's like a Magic 18 Ball," he added, "since *chai* represents the number eighteen." I already knew that because of friends getting bar and bat mitzvah gift checks in multiples of eighteen dollars. "Go ahead. Ask it something," he encouraged.

I hesitated. The last thing I needed was another REPLY HAZY, TRY AGAIN. But then a question came to me. I took a deep breath, closed my eyes, and shook.

I peeked as the response swam into view: YOU CALL THAT A QUESTION?

Rabbi Fred read it over my shoulder and laughed, long and loud. "So much for wisdom, eh?" he said, clapping me on the shoulder. "But I'm glad you stopped by, Noah. I actually have some news to share with you."

"Uh-oh," I said.

"I think you're going to like this news," said Rabbi Fred.

Chapter Sixteen

Noa's party was completely stupid. There were glow sticks, goofy novelty sunglasses, neon fedora hats, a cheesy DJ spinning Top 40 tunes, and a gazillion girls in super-short dresses and mismatched socks dancing to "Cotton Eye Joe."

It was awesome.

Especially when Maya Edelstein asked me to dance and it was a slow song and they turned the lights low and everyone went *"Woooo!"* But she didn't let go, and we kept on dancing, and I think if I had tried to kiss her, she actually might have let me. Plus, almost as good as the possible-kissing part was the fact that it seemed like no one hated me anymore. It was as if by some kind of magic they had all gotten really mature all of a sudden. Or, more likely, they just had other stuff going on, so they had forgotten. Either way, I'd take it.

But even better than that was what happened next.

I was getting a rainbow cup of punch and another rainbow lollipop (for the record, I still hate rainbows in general, but the rainbow lollipops were actually delicious) when I noticed that Dash was at the party. He was across the room, standing by himself, but then Noa ran up to him and put a neon pink fedora on his head. Dash knocked it off, and Noa picked it up and then chased him around the room until a bunch of girls held him down and made him wear it. Every time he took it off, the girls would run up and put it back on him. But he didn't look mad. Clearly, he was enjoying it.

I wasn't going to go talk to him—I'd learned my lesson about that—so I was surprised when he came over to me. And spoke.

"S'up?" he said.

"S'up," I said back. Which was more of a real non-angry conversation than we'd had in months.

"Nice hat," I tried.

"You want it?" he asked, obviously implying that if I took it, the magic would go with it and all the girls would chase me instead of him.

"No, thanks," I said, trying to suggest that I had so much attention from the ladies I couldn't possibly handle any more. Dash set the hat down on a table. I was afraid he was just going to walk away, and I wanted him to stay and hang out so bad I could taste it. I was tempted to grab the hat, put it on, and say something idiotic like "Hey, you know where I got this hat? Mr. Maxx!" Just to make it like old times. Except I had definitely learned my lesson at this point. Those days were gone. And sometimes gone is gone.

But Dash didn't walk off. He stood there, not saying anything, but not leaving, either. Almost like he wanted to be standing next to me. Now, of course I knew better than to say something and ruin the moment. But for me, knowing not to do something and actually resisting the temptation are two completely different things. So I turned to Dash and said, "Hey, is it true what Rabbi Fred told me? That you agreed to share your bar mitzvah date with me?"

Dash shrugged. "It's not until fall. I figured maybe Noa could help us."

My heart was pounding with excitement. I couldn't believe it. Our friendship might not be completely gone after all! It might be mostly dead, but not all dead. And, like Billy Crystal says in *The Princess Bride,* unlike all dead, mostly dead is slightly alive.

"Yeah, Noa did great today," I replied. "It's too bad you missed her speech."

"She already read it to me," said Dash.

"Oh," I said. "Well, she killed up there." I winced at my word choice. "Sorry! I can't help it. I say dumb stuff sometimes."

"Oh, believe me, I know," said Dash.

"Hey," I said indignantly. "You're not exactly Mr. Perfect yourself!"

"Oh yeah?"

"Yeah! You started hating me for, like, no reason. And you started hanging with Noa instead of me. You did, right? I mean, she's CS, isn't she?"

Dash turned bright red, so I knew I had him.

"What does CS stand for, anyway?"

"Curly Stooge," admitted Dash. "But I never hated you."

"You said you did. In your texts to your *girlfriend*."

"She's not my girlfriend," said Dash, though I could tell he was pleased. "Honest, I didn't."

"Yes, you did! You said you 'kind of' hated me."

"Not you, my dad," said Dash.

"You hated your dad?"

"Sometimes," said Dash. "I mean, even though I know his depression was a disease and everything, I still can't help feeling mad and even hating him sometimes. Dr. G, my therapist, says that's okay."

Good, I thought, remembering how I took my own anger and frustration out by kicking Gil's gravestone, and by throwing rocks in the creek, and even by telling off Noa.

Noa.

I suddenly realized something. The look on Noa's face when I said she couldn't really relate to Dash unless her dad had killed himself. I thought I had shocked her by saying that Gil's death had been a suicide. But Dash had already told CS about his father. And CS wasn't Chris. CS was Noa.

So when I said what I said, it wasn't news to Noa. She already knew about Gil. She reacted the way she did not because she was surprised or freaked out by what I said but because she was worried about Dash. She knew he didn't want people to know. And she knew he had only told her.

"You told Noa about your dad?" I finally said. I didn't mean to sound jealous, but I think I might have anyway.

"I mean, yeah. Just her. I didn't want the world to know."

I must have looked pretty upset, because Dash quickly jumped in, saying, "Look, the thing is, Noa never really knew my dad. Not like you did. I know that might not make sense, but it makes it harder for me. Being around you reminds me of being around him. It makes me miss him more."

"Oh," I said. I hadn't thought of that.

"There's other stuff, too," added Dash. "I know everyone thinks he was such a great guy, all happy and joking around, but it wasn't always like that. Sometimes he wasn't even up to letting me have friends over."

"Even me?" I asked.

Dash nodded. "There were times he wouldn't get

out of bed. And he and my mom fought a lot. She thought he needed more treatment. I guess she was right, huh?"

"Yeah."

"My mom says he tried once before," added Dash. "Unsuccessfully, obviously."

I considered telling him that Jenny had already told me that. Given what he'd said about not wanting the whole world to know, playing dumb felt like a better idea. "He did?" I asked.

"Uh-huh. It was before I was born. But when she told me, I felt like I kind of knew already. Weird, huh?"

"Yeah," I agreed. "Did you know he had a gun?"

Dash shook his head. "He didn't," he said. "He must have gotten it for this. Apparently, he planned out the whole thing and made sure me and Pete were at my mom's so we wouldn't be the ones who found him. He even left a note saying he was sorry. Which is another reason I've started to hate apologies."

If he hadn't said that, I probably would have said "I'm sorry." I didn't know what else to say. I could hear the "Cha Cha Slide" song starting up, and I prayed that no one would come over and drag us out on the dance floor now that we were finally talking.

Dash kicked a balloon that had rolled over to us. "Yeah, I'm really the life of the party these days, huh?" he said.

I was trying to just listen and nod, like Enid, but when he said that, I couldn't help responding. "It's not your fault," I told him. "Don't blame yourself." I could hear that I sounded a little like Noa, but hopefully not in a bad way.

"I don't," he said. "I mean, okay, sometimes I do. I'm just all messed up inside. I never used to cry, and now it's like every day. But I don't want people to talk about me. Or feel sorry for me."

I nodded again. I probably looked like the Sandy Koufax bobblehead Rabbi Fred installed in a place of honor next to his lava lamp and Magic 8 . . . er, Jewish Wisdom Ball. I was glad to see the water feature go, but still. Some of his new decor was pretty out there. Though I had to admit that the ball might have had a little magic or wisdom or whatever in it after all.

"Sorry. I didn't mean to dump all that on you," said Dash. "See, there I go. I hate apologies and here I am doing it myself."

"That's okay," I said, appreciating the opportunity to tell him "I'm sorry, too" one more time. I was even more grateful when he changed the subject and said, "Hey, that video montage you did for the cabaret was pretty awesome."

"Thanks!" I said. "Actually, I found this other video you might want to see. It's just an old home movie, but it's got your dad in it."

"Seriously?"

"Uh-huh."

"Cool, I'd like that," said Dash.

Just then, Noa ran up to us with another neon

fedora and slammed it onto Dash's head. "Gotcha!" she yelled. "Now both of you have to report to the dance floor. They're going to do the chair thing."

"Whatever you say, Curly," said Dash, smirking.

"Wait a second, if she's Curly, who does that make me?" I asked.

"You're obviously Larry," said Dash. "I'm Moe."

"How come you get to be Moe?"

"Oh, like you're Moe?"

"Wise guy, eh?"

"Soitainly!"

Our Stooge'ing was quickly drowned out. The music swelled and everyone started clapping when Noa, shrieking and clasping her hands tightly around the edge of the chair's seat, was hoisted into the air. Her red hair bounced all over the place as she was lifted and lowered repeatedly along with the music. I fell in between Maya and Dash and was, for once, grateful for all that grapevine practice.

We wove through the room in intersecting circles while strobe lights flashed and Noa went up and down on her throne. Then they lowered her and lifted her mom up in the chair next, and Noa thrust herself between me and Dash, with Maya still on my other side. I could feel their hands and my hands and our hearts and our feet like one big clumsy caterpillar stepping side, forward, side, back, again and again. All of us laughing, twisting, and, as we danced faster and faster, tripping and inevitably falling like so many drops of rain.

And it was just like Woody Allen says (forgive me, Woody, because I'm paraphrasing here). Even if dancing makes you cringe and you're the king of the remedial grapevine, the song is going to be over much too quickly. So the only thing to do is get up off the floor, grab your fellow Stooges by the hand, and keep on going.

Which is exactly what we did.

Author's Note

When my younger daughter was six, her best friend's father took his own life. In the sad days that followed the initial shock, I watched the two girls play and felt relieved that they were too young to do anything but resume their games, as if nothing had happened. A close friend of mine had lost, at twelve, her mother to suicide, and I knew that for older kids, the immediate impact on their interpersonal relationships could be more complicated. I also knew that for every Dash—and my heart goes out to them—there are a lot of Noahs. That's why I wanted to tell this particular story, and to tell it from Noah's perspective.

In researching this book, I did a lot of reading—about depression, about parental suicide, and about grief and healing. I was fortunate to find some excellent resources, many of which are listed after this note. I was particularly lucky to discover the Wendt Center for Loss and Healing and to have the opportunity to volunteer at Camp Forget-Me-Not/Camp Erin DC. This grief camp is provided free of charge to children and teens who have lost a parent or close family member. All activities are focused on helping the campers grieve and process their loss—through art, sports, talking, theater . . . even banging on drums in the woods. It was at camp that I truly learned just how diverse kids' range of emotions and expressions of grief could be.

I also researched comedy, with a particular focus on Jewish comedy. I can't say I watched every Three Stooges film (far from it—there are over two hundred!), but I tried to reference and include as many Jewish comedy stars and classic comedy bits as I could. If they're not familiar to you, what are you waiting for? Look them up and enjoy!

In closing, I have one thing to say on the subject of writing a book that's simultaneously about something as silly as the Three Stooges and as serious as suicide. Kevin Breel, a comedian and the author of *Boy Meets Depression: Or Life Sucks and Then You ~~Die~~ Live*, provided what I feel is the best explanation for why this juxtaposition is not coincidental. He observed that the definition of laughter is "the tangible evidence of hope." Laughter, even—and perhaps especially—in times of pain and loss, is a force that has the power to connect us, restore us, and urge us forward.

Acknowledgments

To the teenage and adult survivors of parental (and spousal) loss through suicide who generously agreed to talk with me about their experiences, you have my profound thanks. I hope I was able to honor your words and feelings in the pages of this book. I am also grateful to Stephanie Handel, Pamela Lieber, and everyone at both the Wendt Center for Loss and Healing and Camp Forget-Me-Not/Camp Erin DC. Thank you to my fellow blue (volunteer) and red (licensed therapist) shirts, and, most importantly, the amazing campers for all you shared with me and taught me. Group Nine, I will carry your beads with me, always. Thanks also to Ashley Forman and the dedicated Arena Stage Voices of Now team.

I have great appreciation for the rabbis and staff of Temple Micah, in Washington, D.C., who allowed me to be a fly on the wall so that I might capture the people, the place, the humor, and the *ruach*! To all the kids who are wondering if they are in this book: even if you don't see your name in it, you are. Thanks also to Jenny Allen and Karen Kalat, whose first names *are* in the book, though let me assure them and you that this is a work of fiction.

Thanks to Erin Clarke, for being demanding and fearless, as all great editors are. Thanks to Carrie Hannigan, for understanding the story I was trying to write even before I did. Thanks to the wonderful team at Knopf/RHCB, as well as the fabulous librarians and teachers and booksellers and other passionate book people who will get it into the hands of readers. Thanks to my beloved Nerdy Book Club, SCBWI, Children's Book Guild, #WeNeedDiverseBooks, VCCA, DCCAH, First Book, and DMV Women Writers communities—I am honored to know so many awesome and talented folks and to have your friendship and support. And speaking of friends, special thanks to my extreme runner pals—including Clover and Penny—for refusing to let me take myself too seriously or sit too long in one place.

Last but certainly not least, thank you to my family, especially Mike, Franny, and Bougie. Without your love and encouragement (and more-than-occasional noogies), there would be no *Stooges,* or any other book. Everything I do, everything I am, is thanks to you.

Supportive Resources Related to Suicide, Bereavement, and Healing

Suicide Prevention

American Association of Suicidology: suicidology.org
The mission of the AAS is to promote the understanding and prevention of suicide and to support those who have been affected by it.

Crisis Text Line: crisistext.org or text HOME to 741741
When you reach out to the Crisis Text Line, a trained crisis counselor will respond.

Bereavement Support and Healing

The Dougy Center: dougy.org
The mission of the Dougy Center, based in Portland, Oregon, is to provide support in a safe place where children, teens, young adults, and their families grieving a death can share their experiences. Their support group model has been replicated all over the world.

The Moyer Foundation's Camp Erin: moyerfoundation.org/camps-programs/camp-erin
Camp Erin is the largest national bereavement program for youth grieving the death of a significant person in their lives. The Moyer Foundation partners with community-based organizations (including the Wendt Center) to support camps that bring hope and healing to thousands of grieving children and teens each year.

The Wendt Center for Loss and Healing: wendtcenter.org
The Washington, D.C.–based Wendt Center provides an array of holistic services for children, teens, adults, and families seeking to rebuild a sense of safety and hope after experiencing a loss, life-threatening illness, violence, or other trauma. In addition to many other services, the Wendt Center also partners with Arena Stage's Voices of Now program to build teen ensembles that explore issues related to grief and loss through theater (as Noa does in this book). arenastage.org/education/voices-of-now

Winston's Wish: winstonswish.org.uk
A U.K.–based organization dedicated to supporting grieving children and their families.

Support Groups (In-Person and Online)

Alliance of Hope for Suicide Loss Survivors: allianceofhope.org

American Foundation for Suicide Prevention's Find a Support Group: afsp.org/find-support/ive-lost-someone/find-a-support-group

Parents of Suicides/Friends and Families of Suicides: pos-ffos.com

Survivors of Loved Ones to Suicide: solossurvivorsoflovedonestosuicide.com

Books

NOTE: *These books all contain lists of resources for families and children coping with loss. In addition, the Dougy Center website (dougy.org) offers a selection of free and affordable resources: books, brochures, DVDs, and streaming video, as well as Dougy Center podcasts.*

Hughes, Lynne B. *You Are Not Alone: Teens Talk About Life After the Loss of a Parent.* New York: Scholastic, 2005.

Requarth, Margo. *After a Parent's Suicide: Helping Children Heal.* Sebastopol, CA: Healing Hearts Press, 2006.

Rubel, Barbara. *But I Didn't Say Goodbye: Helping Children and Families After a Suicide.* Kendall Park, NJ: Griefwork Center, 2009.

Some (of the Many) Comedians Who Have Spoken Openly About Depression

I have been struck by how many prominent comedians have spoken candidly about their struggles with depression. Arguably, it might have been easier to create a list of comedians who have *not* gone on record about this topic. I decided instead to provide a short list of comedians who either have found ways to incorporate this important topic into their work or have been particularly brave in addressing a subject that is, certainly, no laughing matter.

Wayne Brady	Paul Gilmartin
Kevin Breel	Marc Maron
Neal Brennan	Aparna Nancherla
Jim Carrey	Joan Rivers
Chris Gethard	Sarah Silverman